BREATHE

BREATHE

DASH STARKEY

www.dashstarkey.com

ISBN:
Paperback
978-0-6487919-0-4
Digital Media
978-0-6487919-1-1

Editor: Tegan O'Gorman

First Printing, 2021

All of my books are dedicated to
Love and Life
... I hope you find yours.

Elle, my love and my life.

Gratitude
My baby girl **Emily**, the light of my life.
My parents, **Cliff and Heather**, for
their amazing love and
encouragement.
Tegan O'Gorman a talented editor and
author.

~ 1 ~

Moments suck. They really do. And it is generally those minor insignificant moments which you barely notice that can flip your life on its head. With headache inducing thought I try to place the very moment it all changed, not a minor shift, a complete life altering moment where my life, as I knew it, vanished and a new one replaced it. For better or for worse. Its as if I threw a dice in the air and whatever number it landed on would become the direction of my life, and not just any ordinary six-sided dice but a twenty-sided one. I can't even fathom my life having the ability to head in twenty different directions, it could apparently.

I try to place my finger on it, the elusive moment. I back track from where I stand now to where I thought I stood. One moment pops up frequently though I dismiss it. Can a mere sentence be moment enough? Not just a sentence, a tiny, oh ever so tiny, white lie? How could that impact a life so drastically that everything you thought that you were, that you stood for and that was enclosed in your very soul, could change? Is that possible or have I just been ignorant all my life.

I'm sure you're wondering about my 'special' moment however there is not much to it. I lied to my mother. Yep that was the start of the end of my life as I knew it. Little did I know a new reality awaited me barely moments after I uttered the fateful words, 'Mum I am in a relationship, with a woman.'

It's quite laughable really, how such a lie escaped my mouth. My life was going nowhere, I had a dead-end job and to be honest I thought I was sort of happy. Life lacked pizzazz and I truthfully had no personal life beyond a handful of friends. Isn't that happiness in today's busy world?

Worst of all I work in an English style pub. You know the type of place. Dark and broody on the outside. Plenty of timber panelling and wooden window frames where the amber light drizzles out like honey. And even though I live in a very humid and warm city, I feel cold shivers whenever I stare into those windows. The amber hue makes it look like everyone is cosy inside, huddled by a fire, while I stand alone in the dreary grey of an imagined English winter.

Most English pubs are named after contrasting and unimaginable combinations like 'The Elephant and Wheelbarrow', 'The Jolly Taxpayer' and 'The Cat and Custard Pot'. Not fully following tradition, this pub is still a combination that makes one think about who the hell would name a place that.

Simply known as Hot Rocks, the place is named, I assume, after the searing hot stones used to serve sizzling steaks. That is what I tell people. Though if you consider that the gay chef and owner, JoJo, has the most wicked sense of humour, then it is possible to assume it stands for something else entirely. Very possible.

Inside beyond the rustic bar and brass studded red leather booths the atmosphere is quite tame. It is a relaxed social drinking establishment where food happens to be served. Thankfully it is, otherwise, I wouldn't have a job. Not that serving food is a lifelong dream, but, at this moment, I really can't think of what I want to do with my life. So, I tread water, this life of serving food and scrubbing plates. It is a cycle of rinse and repeat, surely, I am not alone. Many others do the same, not that it justifies my choice, or my lack of choosing. Like a big bowl of fish, we all just swim around, bumping heads and hitting the sidewalls. Going nowhere, being nothing and thinking we are happy.

Hot Rocks has been referred to as many things. Some reviews are scathing, yet those who come here aren't about image and such. Basically, you belong if you like to chug beer and your perception on love is somehow ... bent!

Take Tex for example. Our souvenir from senior year. A few of us travelled to the Tamworth Country Music Festival expecting to return with a lousy t-shirt or two, maybe a story to tell, instead we returned with Tex.

We found Tex when we arrived in Tamworth and entered a classic Australian country town pub, our first, ready to take on whatever presented itself. Like most pubs there was a well-worn bar with local brews labelled on brass taps, vinyl covered stools and peanuts in ashtrays laid spaciously apart on the beer-soaked bar mat. Recent laws banning smoking inside establishments now made these ashtrays mere ornaments. A faint breeze, combined with a stench of manure, flowed gently through a line of open windows which sat either side of the double wide entry doors. An assortment of mismatched chairs sat around equally mismatched tables; all were empty. The reason being that all the patrons were crammed around a raised table near one particular window. Loud cheering emitted from the crowd.

Within the circle was Tex, wearing blue jeans, a white sleeveless shirt and a black Akubra. Next to her was a very solidly built man in jeans and a blue singlet with hair escaping every part of unexposed skin on his shoulders and back. Both participants held a shot glass full of tequila. The crowd yelled 'thirteen' as the pair threw back the shot until the slightly golden liquid vanished down their throats. Tex had picked up the next while the man swayed slightly. As he picked up the glass the crowd yelled 'fourteen' and Tex had thrown it back quicker than the previous. The man tried although as his head tilted backwards his body followed in a slow motion, Matrix kind of way. As he hit the floor, she picked up some cash, and bounced over to us. That's how we met Tex.

Looking at her now I don't think anyone ever really knew her proper name. It didn't matter much as she was the sort men drooled over and straight women wanted to sleep with. Her tight leather pants showed the exact volume of her arse, and her vest top? Well, we will just say everyone waited in anticipation of them bursting free. You always knew when Tex entered the bar as she always turned heads. I'd be taking an order when suddenly the customer I was talking to would swivel their head away from me, exorcist style, so you just knew. That, or you could hear whispers of bravado and daring's amongst the booths filled with hopeful suitors. Tex's boots would jingle in the still air. I think she glued small bells into the heels though she denies this adamantly. And Tex didn't just walk, she floated in long seductive strides. Strides and seductive may sound contradictive, on her it worked. It was a sultry, I just got off a horse, sort of stride.

'I tell you.' Even her voice had a slight twang to it. 'Commitment's not for me. No one's going to lasso this little filly.'

'Who will you share those special moments with?' Prompts Clare.

'Plenty!' Tex's eyes always lit up when she bantered with Clare. Her laughter filled the eatery. Those who hadn't noticed her before, were drawn to the seductiveness of that laugh now.

Backing down wasn't in Clare's vocabulary. 'What happens when you get older? Have you any idea how you will look back on your life ten years from now?

'Baby, I'm Tex Colbert, the best frigging photographer any of the men's magazines have had. I sleep with women that men only dream about. When I'm old I will have plenty to look back on, maybe even have an indecent picture or two.'

With that comment, I nearly spilled their drinks. Tex continued, pleased at her endeavour to make Clare, and myself, feel uncomfortable.

'The young girls will be swarming all over me. Each wanting to become more famous than the last. And let me tell you, fame has a price!' Her devilish grin enveloped her face as she leant forward daring Clare to continue.

Standing poised to take their food order, I waited silently. Clare huffed as she often did. I fidgeted as I often did.

'Your looks won't always be there, nor your camera.'

'Then they will just be wanting me for my money or my bedroom skills. Either is fine.'

'Your head is getting way too big for this booth. How can you live with yourself? Using those poor girls. No no.' Waving her hand, Clare momentarily silences Tex. 'Don't use the excuse they are using you. In years to come, will you be able to recollect these choices with satisfaction?'

And there, ladies and gentlemen, is another character in the Hot Rocks assortment. Clare, the unofficial conscience of the place. It's funny, I always think of her when I see a flower delivery dude with a bouquet of helium balloons. I see the faces of my friends in each balloon, except for Clare's. Her face sits on the marble bag that all the strings are attached to. Our rock, keeping it all together, keeping us all together.

In a horror movie Clare would be the person who didn't want to go into the dark woods. The one who disagreed with the practicality of the whole plan and thus was killed or eaten first. To be honest I would probably be second.

Her childhood in Ascot could only be described as normal, her accountancy job stable, her relationship enduring. I always found it weird that we shared a dorm for 5 years at a private school only two blocks from her parent's house, I never asked why. My situation was different, of course, for my parents lived on a property one hundred and twenty-two point five kilometres outside of Rockhampton. Never forget the point five for it makes a world of difference between a land of nothing, and a place of, well, nothing. We all had common ground, even though we all came from differing backgrounds, even Harry. Harry lived in a rundown unit at Redcliffe, raised by a single mother who had plenty of male visitors.

Harry, these days, is one of those big magazine editors that gets invited to all the best parties. Parties attended by people you normally only see on glossy magazines. A flashy dresser, Harry wears tailored suits and chunky gold jewellery. Oh, did I tell, Harry is short for Harriette. That's right she's a girl, a woman, some may even say a dyke, though labels lose some of the essence of a person. Especially with Harry.

Although Harry went to a state school, and was given fewer opportunities, she managed to educate herself and success followed rapidly. I suppose it is one of those real rags to riches stories. She has skills, those too but ones that can make her money. You know what I mean, writing skills. Her written words are second to none. She used to write letters to regional newspapers and her local council in regard to issues she felt were important. She was always published or received a positive response. In one instance she actually got the council to change their policies because her letter was so detailed, full of facts and solutions, and sounded like they came from someone with great experience.

Ask anyone and they will all say that there is no greater

love in Harry's life than Clare. It's amazing that they have been together for so long. Since high school. I remember how they met, it's quite funny really. We were playing field hockey against Redcliffe High School. Harry was their goalkeeper while Clare was the main goal scorer for our side. The game was coming down to the final minutes and Clare made a break. Her concentration on the ball was to such an extent she never looked up and WHAM! She collided with Harry's helmet. Next thing you know Clare's unconscious. What a way to start a relationship. By the way, we lost, if anyone cares.

People at Hot Rocks try to imitate the success of their relationship. Or at least the durability. After fifteen years they still hold hands in public and they refer to one another's recollection of the past as though it were a common memory bank. Not only are these two women comfortable together, the very presence of each is comforting to the other, as well as to us dreamers. Finding a soul mate that young must be amazing.

'Honey don't get started with Tex again. You know she likes to play with you. Jilly's here to take our order.'

I like the way Harry gestures to me; it enforces my existence. I pretend not to notice Harry caressing Clare's hand as Tex pretends to lose interest in the game.

'So Tex, who's this month's centrefold?' Harry and her sly smile re-ignite the situation.

'Harry!' From birth Clare was wound too tight. I'm sure of it.

'It's for the magazine.' Harry protested although she laughed with us.

'You're quiet today Gill, what's up?'

Other than the use of my non-name, there was no other indication that Tex was talking to me. In fact, she was positioning the girls, her cleavage, so that the boys at the next table could view them at an advantageous angle.

'You know. Just mother trouble.'

'It's always your mum Gill.'

My desire was to inform Tex to either use my full name Gillian or the shorter Jilly. For I hated Gill as it reminded me of … a fish. Well a fish's breathing apparatus. I often wondered if she used it because of my anxiety and the way I often mumbled to myself to just breathe because that was the only thing that came close to calming me. True she took the first four letters of my full name; it was the way she pronounced it. It was just wrong. Though to inform her of this would have just given her more incentive to use the stupid version.

Well anyway, Tex's plan must have worked because the bar waitress brought over a drink sent from the other table. Tex raised it high in a thank-you and sculled it in one fluid motion. The cheers and scuffle from the boys indicated another drink may be on the way. At this moment I wished for one, or two, or more.

'She still hounding you about getting married?'

Clare was always sympathetic, or maybe I was always pathetic. Don't know. I did my darndest to ignore the question, Clare grabbed my arm as I turned towards the kitchen, mumbling a response. More to my chest than to anyone.

'What was that mate?' Tex waved to the boys, so they'd send even more drinks.

'I told her I couldn't get married cause I was living with a woman.'

I felt the heat rise from deep within, right up my neck until it flooded my face.

'And that's stopping your dating?' Scoffed Harry.

'You don't mean?' Clare's eyes looked up at me, searching my very soul. I was stuck to the spot. 'You're straight!'

Well I know that. The words flow easily through my head; never out of my mouth. Instead I give a dumb fish caught in a bowl look.

'Hell, we all know that.' Stated Harry.

The response was simultaneous. Tex practically choked on her second drink, or third, I wasn't keeping count. Clare flung a hand over her gaping mouth. Fortunately, Harry was the only one to see the humour in the situation. She thumped the table with her hand and let out a deep baritone laugh.

'I always knew you'd switch sides.' Harry seemed delighted in the prospect. 'Here sign this so you can have a free toaster oven.'

Someone wants to give me a toaster oven? Is that a crack at me?

'Nine more signatures and I get a free set of steak knives!'

Yes, definitely a crack. Part of her conversion score I suppose.

'So, Gill. You've been holding out on us or aren't we

good enough for you? Not your type?' Tex could barely contain herself.

'Who is this mystery woman you have failed to tell us about?'

Tex had completely forgotten about the free drinks. If I was a wild lioness, I would have snarled at her. I wasn't. So, I didn't. I was thankful to Clare for distracting me from Tex. Then again it was the ever-questioning Clare.

'Well Jilly, a lie will only hold her off for a short period.'

And here is where my real dilemma starts. Mother had taken the news as could be expected.

'The problem is.'

And what a problem. It had all been so easy when the words slid effortlessly from my mouth down the telephone line to my mother in Rockhampton, well one hundred and twenty-two point five kilometres outside of Rockhampton. My parents shipped me to Brisbane to have a proper education. Naturally when school finished, I stayed. More opportunities I told them. Besides how could I leave friends like these? Right now, it appeared very easy.

'Just breathe Jilly. You can say it.'

Ever so supportive Clare. She understood anxiety and stressful situations. How these situations always found me I will never know.

'She wants to come and meet this so-called girlfriend that she has heard so little about. She arrives Sunday.'

Their eyes bulged. It was Friday now. Darting back to the kitchen before they could say another word, I gasped for breath. For some reason the room became blurry as if it was spinning at one hundred miles an hour. When I finally managed to see clearly again, I saw my posse of friends with their heads huddled. Tex and Harry laughed merrily while Clare spoke earnestly. It was disappointing when their meals were ready.

'Okay little lady.' Harry had me cornered between her, Clare and the table. 'Who have you selected for this mission? Anyone we know?'

'Not a complete stranger!' Interjected Clare.

'Well.'

Someone was in my mind. Unthinkingly I gazed at Tex, my mouth opened and closed. I felt like the fish in the fishbowl again, now there was no water.

'ME? No frigging way!' Tex's face was distorted. Torn between horror and humour.

So, there you are. Another emotional tangle to sort out. At first glance it appeared that I had placed little thought into this lie. That would be true. Why else would anyone, namely me, pick the most adventurous seductress out there to play a loving partner? In between service I tried to explain. It was hard. The lie was to give me some breathing room from a mother who was insistent that a woman's biological clock would expire exactly on midnight of her 35th birthday. And since courtship took anything up to three years, I was hanging perilously on the edge of expiration. Apparently.

'Mum was pushing for me to meet up with her friend's son Jack the lawyer. I can just see her vision now of a big fancy wedding and soon afterwards me with a baby on each hip and one around my ankles. It was too much.'

I let out a huge sigh. How many disastrous blind dates had my mother already cursed me with?

'I'm out.' Declared Tex followed by 'I'm off to The Horny Toad to find a real meaningful relationship.'

'A one-night stand more likely,' bellowed Harry behind her.

Tex gave us the thumbs up signal then vanished.

Yes, I'd known these three for a long time. At times I felt the odd one out. They were sporty and adventurous and lesbians. I wasn't any of these things. I used to stand in my room alone, looking in the long mirror at my disproportioned body. Turning this way and that. If only my boobs were this much bigger, my arse that much smaller. I'd even considered becoming gay if that made me more interesting. It wouldn't. So, I didn't.

My world was in turmoil, my friends continued as per normal. What could I expect from people not hanging on the edge of expiration? Maybe my uterus was like yoghurt. Hit that special date then became green fuzzy stuff. Or worse still, how mother was right and at midnight on my 35th birthday it just vanished, never to be seen again. Just breathe.

~ 2 ~

It would have been selfish of me to think that I was all my friends thought about. In truth, they had their own lives and their own problems.

'You coming to bed Harry?' Clare stood in the doorway framed by light.

'Soon.' Startled, Harry closed the tab she was working on. 'I have some work to do on the computer.' Her hand shook as she poured another glass of whiskey.

'It's kinda funny.'

'What is Clare?' Harry turned to her wife annoyed by the interruption. Her eyes flashed over Clare's rubber ducky covered pyjamas. They used to be cute.

'You used to wrestle me to the bed.' A mischievous grin filled Clare's face. She missed the passion their relationship once had. The spontaneity.

'As enjoyable as that may be, I have work.'

'Work. That's all you have lately. Work, staying out late and drinking. Again.' Clare loved Harry as much as the day they met, lately, she didn't feel a priority to her wife, and that is why she had the hurt tone in her voice.

'You know how much pressure I'm under Clare.' Harry was frustrated. She felt frustrated a lot lately.

Clare leant in closer. 'Sure, work. Now come show me

what you were hiding.' Smiling Clare playfully tapped the mouse trying to bring up the reduced screen. 'Is it porn?'

'No!' Harry did not want to explain herself nor did she feel she deserved judgement.

The screen blinked into existence. Clare's eyes scanned it briefly. Harry slammed the power button so the screen blackened from the outer limits first and the evidence vanished to a small central dot before popping away.

'What was that? A chatroom?' A confused look infused Clare's face. She reached for the mouse again.

'No!'

The slap was swift. Stinging where Harry's hand had landed. Rising from the chair Harry took Clare by surprise. Unbalanced by the slap, Clare stepped backwards. Her face was full of incomprehension. Tears welled and slowly spilt down her cheeks.

'Harry?' The word was meek, questioning.

'I said no. Just go to bed.' Shaking her head, Harry kissed Clare's forehead and pushed her towards the bedroom. 'Now. I'll be in shortly.'

Obediently Clare retreated to the ensuite in the adjoining bedroom. She washed her face, sniffled, and washed her face again. Tentatively her hand drifted over the spot. THE spot. It was warm and red. Familiar too. As Clare looked up from the third washing, she saw Harry's reflection in the mirror.

Embracing her from behind, Harry whispered the words 'I'm sorry' into Clare's ear.

'Yes. I'm sorry too.' Clare wiggled, Harry's strong arms kept her in place. 'You promised.'

'I know.'

'Are you cheating on me?' The eyes in the mirror met, Clare's were red and puffy. Harry's, as of late, were made of steel.

'No. Do we have to do this dance again?' Harry's arms released. The conversation would go nowhere other than pissing her off.

'Why then?'

'Damn Clare. Can't you just give me some space? I'm always smothered by you.'

'How Harry? How do I smother you? Do I love you too much? Do I care too much? Do I let you drink too much? Please tell me.' The words were sharp, they forced Harry to the bedroom.

'You expect too damn much from me. I'm not your mother, I'm not your father. They may treat you like a spoilt little princess, that ain't my job.' The pitch of the words rose as did Harry's anger.

'A spoilt little princess? Is that all I am?' Clare couldn't help herself, she pushed further. 'Or are you jealous? Jealous that they provided me with what your parents couldn't. Shelter, food, love.'

'Fuck you Clare.' Harry's hands clenched into fists.

'No. You have made a success of your life, still you carry on with this sorry little act about unfortunate you, how long do I have to hear about it?' Clare turned to sit on the bed. This wasn't her; this wasn't how their relationship should be. 'How long?'

'Yeah,' replied Harry in a tone filled with anger.

No other words had a chance to leave Clare's mouth for

Harry's fist swung round so sharply it caught her jaw. The force threw her flat on to the bed. Harry was on top now. Every time Clare went to speak, Harry slapped her again. Finally, exhausted, with tears rolling down both of their faces, Harry slid to the side. Clare sobbed unashamedly. Harry embraced her and brought her close.

'Oh baby, I'm so sorry. It's just, you know. You keep pushing me. You know that makes me aggro.' Harry peppered her face with kisses. 'You just need to stop pushing.'

There are many forms of wrestling with a lover. Tex never turned down a promising opportunity. Her attitude about entering a relationship was that you could make it as casual or as complicated as you desired. Casual generally won. Actually it won every time, especially if you classed twelve hours or less as casual.

The Horny Toad was her club of choice. It was the most happening gay bar in town. The décor by night looked far more appealing than by the daylight. If you were still standing here by daylight you were absolutely doing something wrong as this was a guaranteed pick up bar.

The entrance way was made up of large aluminium framed glass doors that slid open to create an unobstructed view, and access, to the Valley's open-air pedestrian mall. Great for drawing people in or throwing them out.

Small tables scattered this outer area, where the club served food and alcohol. During the early evening hours, it felt more like a café than a club. Groups would often meet here before taking on a night of fun. The bar that served this area was set back in the building enough to provide space for indoor tables though not too far for a drunk to stumble. High above the bar on the back mirror was a bright green neon sign of what looked more like a slick green tree frog, than a bumpy dry toad, albeit it had a neon purple horn on its head. The mirror behind the sign made it brighter and projected the colours across the space in front of the bar. Odd yet effective in enhancing the mood.

Mirror image to this bar was an identical one behind it. It was identical in every manner right down to the green frog with a purple horn on its head. Though this side had less lighting giving it a darker, edgier feel. Not a bad thing considering what some of the patrons got up to. For those who wanted to do more than drink, there was a selection of areas: a dance floor, an upper mezzanine with pool tables and a karaoke station which didn't generally kick off till later in the night.

Tex liked this place especially the bartender James who was friendly and attentive to his patron's alcoholic needs. She felt he foresaw her need for a drink before she did. It was a true skill.

'You're a devil Tex.' James hands her another drink. 'What about the one dancing on the pool table. Mmm Mmm. One major hottie that one.'

Tex huffs in laughter. 'She's cute Jimmy, more your type than mine.'

James blushes a little. Yes, he did like the good girls gone bad - for just one night - look.

'So why does a straight man work in a gay bar? Are you secretly gay? Or do you love rejection?'

It was true James was straight. By day he worked as a tradesman and to be honest he made good money, still he wanted more. He developed bar skills in his father's country pub. A place full of roughnecks, homophobes and just plain hard-working people. Sure, he could have got a bar job anywhere, surprisingly he loved the atmosphere here, the tips too but most of all, when he moved to the city, he just wanted to step out of his comfort zone and experience life.

'Rejection I suppose.'

James smiles as he scans the bar to anticipate the needs of his customers. A quick scotch here, an old-style grasshopper cocktail there and a quick wave to the bouncer to prevent a possible misunderstanding at the pool tables.

James likes Tex. He didn't like being called Jimmy as that was what the people at home called him. In the city he wanted to be more than that country boy. He saw the country in her too and that's probably why they bonded so well.

'How's about the one lounging on the couch.' Tex was scanning for a quick pick up. The Horny Toad had never failed to supply.

'Oh. Not that one. She already has a companion. And by the look of her, she has more balls than I do.' Filling up her empty glass, James shook his head. 'I bet you will strike out.'

'How much do you bet?' The girl's companion rose and left for the toilet. 'Look again Jimmy. An open target.'

'I'd wager a 50 you won't get to her in time and if you do, she'll say no.'

'Just fifty dollars for a challenge like this?' Tex smirked.

'You know you're losing time. Yes, a 50, plus when you strike out, I'll make you sing karaoke, Islands in the Stream, with Reggie.'

Reggie, a resident feature of The Horny Toad, was a not so feminine drag queen with a voice like gravel who loved to sing karaoke especially a duet. James chuckled to himself.

'Challenge accepted. You should know me better by now Jimmy.' Tex made her move. She slithered through the crowd and approached the girl sitting by herself. 'Here. You look thirsty.' A wink accompanied the drink.

There is no need to say what occurred next before that girl's companion reappeared. Tex played her well-rehearsed smooth moves. Soon she had the girl on her arm heading out of the club. Thankfully the bar was on their way.

'And we score Jimmy. You owe me $50 so I'll catch you later.' Tex's words were mocking.

'You won a football bet?' Asked the girl on Tex's arm.

Jimmy laughed and shook his head while Tex just smiled and said 'Yep.'

The girl's companion returned from the toilet, paused at the couch then let her eyes search the room. There was nothing to find. No matter if you have steel balls or titanium ovaries, there is nothing you can do with an empty couch.

I only wish I was wrestling with a lover, sadly I was left

wrestling with my lies. The chef, JoJo, and I worked past closing time preparing the kitchen for the morning. JoJo was the flamboyant type that believed he could construct any ingredients into a masterpiece. If I gave him the fragments of my life, I wonder if he could create a masterpiece out of them?

'What's up pretty lady? You've looked glum all night.'

JoJo pulled a mockingly sour face as he flung his tea towel to the wash pile and sat on one of the stainless benches. Popping the top off two pre-chilled beers, his expression was serene, that was normal for him.

'I told my mother I was living with a woman, as in a relationship. You know how much she nags me to settle down. I thought it'd slow her down.'

The corners of JoJo's lips curled ever so slightly, he said nothing. Nodding his head gently JoJo's eyes lit up with what I assumed was excitement. Excited because I lied to my mother or for the story itself, I was initially unsure.

'And I said Tex was my partner.' I continued scrubbing the bench.

'Tex!' The beer sprayed from his mouth and nostrils simultaneously. His eyes connected with mine. 'Girl, you should have picked someone easier.'

Tell me about it. Mother Teresa would have been easier.

'Well I didn't think it would matter. It was only a story.'

'And now?'

As his eyes lit up further, I'm sure he was enjoying this too much. Did he enjoy watching me squirm or did he enjoy me cleaning his benches to a brilliance brighter than the sun.

'Have you spoken to Tex?'

'I really didn't think it would come to that. Mum's arriving Sunday to make sure it's, well, real. Or to prove me wrong in the lie. Oh, I don't know. Maybe she thinks we're just good friends?'

The emphasis on good. I should have just told her I had kidney disease or something easy like that. No, I had to deal the gay card.

'Okay. Well there are three options as I can see it,' said JoJo as his hands unconsciously turned a skimpy paper serviette into a beautiful swan. 'Have someone play a woman named Tex except your mum met Tex at your graduation. Or ask that womanising hussy. Or tell your mother the truth! It's that simple.'

People tell lies all the time. We all do it. Some are little white lies meant to protect. Others are evil dark lies meant to hurt. This lie wasn't created to hurt anyone, especially not me. Like most lies, they don't stay small. Lies are like weeds. Give them a little air, a little bullshit and they blossom. And one day they take over the whole yard, or your life. Whichever comes first.

JoJo's final words were no help, at all. 'Good luck girl, you're going to need it.'

Sink or swim. I'd slept late. Ate nothing as my stomach was doing flips. And proceeded to the docks where Tex lived in a warehouse converted. It looked condemned. Tex liked the rustic look of the old wooden building. She said it gave her space for her photography and her mind. That and the photographic props were great turn ons for some women. The thought of these women crosses my mind now. Near naked women and props. This has my head hurting already. Just breathe. The knock I rap on the door is weak and hesitant. In truth I hope Tex is not home. Not that it would help my dilemma, realistically it would allow me to flee. Unfortunately, Tex answers the door. My throat goes dry as she stands before me in leather chaps, a cowboy hat and spurs. Nothing else!

'Really? You answer the door like that?'

I avert my eyes trying not to look directly at her nakedness. I raise my hand to make it easier.

Tex is surprised to see me. 'Oh, it's you.'

She turns and heads towards the coffee machine, flippantly swinging a robe over her shoulders on the way. I follow with hesitation trying to rise saliva into my dry mouth.

'Can you put those things away?'

Tex wraps the robe tighter about her.

'Jilly the answer is no.'

Hey, she used a preferred derivative of my name!

'Please. Please. Please.' The last please was drawn out. 'I will owe you big time.'

Well, I'm not ashamed to say that I pleaded my case. Practically got down on my knees and begged. I'm not proud of the fact. All I got in return was the same one syllable word.

'No.'

Finally, she realised this answer would not satisfy me.

'Jilly, why did you pick me? Of all the people you know, I am the least committing. To be honest your Mum probably knows that too. Even if you've only told her half of our group's adventures. I run by the seat of my pants and love it. And most importantly have you ever seen me hold down a relationship for longer than a week, a day, an hour even? I'm really not good at it. I'm not designed for it.'

Her arms were raised in emphasis however with the sunlight streaming in the window behind her, she looked like an angel. An angel ready for flight. The cowboy hat, her halo. Damn you Tex.

'Well this is just a fake relationship. It's only for a couple of days, no more.' What could be easier, I think.

'I'm not good at fake ones either.'

I splurt a laugh: Tex glares me down. I take a breath and try to hold it together.

'You are the most courageous person I know. You are self-assured, confident, adventurous, and funny. Everything I'm not.'

'Really you think that? Hmm I be thinking Gilly wants me. Gilly needs me.'

Now I just want to punch her face. How was I going to word this?

'Me. Men don't even see me when I walk by, you, oh, both men and women notice you.'

'That's bull Jilly.'

Tex moved towards the open kitchen while I moved towards that warming sunlight.

'You are like everyone's dream which means you'll never be lonely. Do you know what lonely is Tex?'

The warmth felt nice. It embraced me, bolstering my confidence.

'Sure, there are friends to fill in the between times, the other times, those quiet moments, can swallow you up.'

'You should get down to The Horny Toad. No quiet moments there.' The words flowed over the lip of a steaming coffee cup.

'Damn you Tex. How long have we been friends? All I'm asking is for you to help me out. Didn't I have your back that time we were in Launceston? And Perth? And come to think of it, Bondi? Did I bail on you? No. Was it comfortable? Not in the slightest, that is what friends do. We are friends, aren't we?'

My little speech must have frightened her. Tex approached me from behind and rubbed my back. It felt nice. Her emotional barometer barely ever moved so I didn't expect this sign of understanding. The tone of her words hadn't changed from normal.

'You've had more enduring romances than me. When my romance disappears, I get dressed and leave.'

Tex was being funny. I wasn't. My head hangs limp.

'I'm not as free-spirited as you. Soul mates are hard to find. I just need time. Breathing space. Look, I'm lonely Tex and I'm afraid I will be for the rest of my life.'

Turning, I allow the warmth to seep into my back. Tex looks at me curiously.

'And for a few moments in time I don't want to be reminded of that.'

'A fake girlfriend will not fix that.'

'I will never ask for anything again.' Not until I can work out a new plan. Let's be honest here.

'You're straight. I'm a womaniser. How is that going to work?'

'Come on Tex. I'll give you anything. Anything you want.'

'Anything?'

The debate was swaying in my direction, so I pushed harder.

'Yes, anything you want. Anything.'

Tex leant in; her fingers brushed my lips. Surprised I pulled from her touch.

'See! You don't even like my touch and you think your mother is going to buy that we are in love? Geez Gill.'

Time for the closing argument.

'I need you Tex. Please do me this one favour and I will owe you. Simple as that. Anything.'

'Yes.'

It was a straight out yes. I was expecting more of an argument. Maybe a future unknown flashed before her. Understand, this is a big step for Tex as she hasn't lived with anyone since she was sixteen. And parents don't count. Mother was arriving tomorrow, so I had to prevent her backing out.

'Let's get you packed. We've got to go now.'

I cannot let her change her mind! A noise distracted me for a moment. I turned to see a woman walk naked into the kitchen. Tex continued to sip her steaming coffee.

'You got any juice?' The girl asked.

'Yeah, in the fridge.' Tex nodded in the direction of the fridge.

The girl smiled at me and asked if I wanted any juice. It was hard to speak to her and avert my eyes at the same time. In some ways, I felt rude not talking directly to her. For her part she just shrugged, poured a glass, sipped it slowly and returned the bottle to the fridge.

'You seen my clothes?' She asked as she left the room.

'By the hobby horse I think.' Responded Tex without taking her eyes from me.

'You were saying?'

I stumbled over the words. 'We've got to go. Now.'

'Dressed like this?'

Hmmm. That was a point. She was still in her chaps and robe. So courteously I waited till she changed. As I dragged her out the door to my waiting Jeep she yelled to the previously naked woman.

'I gotta go Nat, Cat, Karman ...?'

'Trish.' The girl responded, her voice faint in the distance.

'You let yourself out Trish?'

'Sure.'

'Cheers then.'

The interaction seemed odd to me.

'You're not going to make sure she leaves first?'

'Nah. If I'm not there to entertain her why would she stay?'

'She might steal something?'

'Okay worry wart.'

Tex turns to the open door.

'Hey Trish, can I call you a cab or drop you somewhere?'

I hit Tex in the arm, and she gives me the 'what' look.

'Cab would be great. Umm do you have any money for the cab?'

'Yeah there's a twenty in the bowl by the front door.'

To my 'what' look Tex responds.

'It happens a lot. Worth it really to get rid of them.'

Over the years my weight had fluctuated. It was a struggle, looking at Tex now, throwing her duffel bag in the back, I realise her weight has never changed. Yes, even though she'd grown taller, her body always seemed proportioned correctly. I wonder why she never took to the other side of the camera. It's funny how you can know someone for so long and fail to ask the simplest questions.

'Got everything? Mum'll be here for a few days.'

I look at her as we drive. An absent expression fills her face. My silent curses about her always being unfazed by things went unheard. Barely a word is mumbled on the remainder of the trip. As we pulled into the drive, the sanctuary of my house lay before me. I sat for a moment trying to absorb the last of the peacefulness before my house was invaded. Firstly, by Tex then by my mother.

Tex passes through the front room then proceeds up the stairs. I see her turn right towards my bedroom.

'What are you doing?'

'Moving in.' She pauses for dramatic effect. 'Lover.' The word was breathy and well pronounced.

I ran up the stairs behind her. As she heaves the duffel bag onto the bed, an amused look crosses Tex's face.

'So, where do I put my stuff.'

'Oh.' Heat fills my face. I had not thought about that.

Tex didn't wait for an answer instead she opens my closet and shoves my clothes to one side. Making herself at home she does the same with a dresser drawer then proceeds to fill the spaces with her belongings.

'Can't we put them in the spare room?'

'Wouldn't want me walking in naked on your mother, would you?'

Damn that Cheshire cat grin.

'Naked?' My mouth became dry, and a lump the size of a baseball became lodged in my throat. Just breathe.

'Your mother will be in the spare room. Besides she will be expecting us to be sleeping together, Gill.' The tone was mocking. 'Right side or left? I normally prefer the right. That okay with you lover?'

My head ached from the pain. I could barely stand from the nausea that swept over me. Later that night on the telephone I reported to Clare, my close confidant, that the room had begun to swirl. That and my breath became short and spasmodic whenever Tex said the word lover. Even though there were many second thoughts about the situation, my mother was arriving tomorrow so what could I do? Clare seemed distant but reassured me brunch at her house was still a go.

No matter how hard I wished it wouldn't, the morning arrived on time. It was going to be a beautiful day full of the unknown. I managed to talk Tex into sleeping in the spare room even though she insisted we practice a sleeping ritual. I woke early. Realistically I don't think I slept at all. I crept downstairs as if I was a grounded teenager heading out for the night. The house was still and quiet.

The morning sun touched the edges of the table. I let my fingertips play in the warmth. My thoughts returned to the coffee before me. Simple thoughts. Watching the cream swirl. I stirred it again, the childish game making me smile. At intervals, I dropped more cream in, then stirred. Soon the liquid no longer resembled coffee.

What alerted me to Tex's presence was the patter on the stairs followed by the rattle of the coffee machine. As I turned, she leant against the counter, looking casual as she faced me. One arm lay extended along the bench for balance. The other raised a mug to her mouth.

'Mornin.'

Her smile was warm. What never struck me before was that it was also lopsided. She wore boxers and a singlet probably for my benefit. Under her hat I assumed her hair was tousled. I also wondered if she wore the hat to bed.

As she sat beside me, I studied the creamy liquid that had once been coffee in my mug. In a perverted way it was nice having someone to wake up to. To avoid her studying eyes, I grasped the first question, that rose in my mind.

'What's it like being a lesbian?'

The smile remained firm, Tex's eyes lost some of their gleam. Was the question insulting? I hadn't thought so. There was a brief silence before the answer came.

"What is it like being a heterosexual?'

'What a stupid question.' That really was stupid. 'It is like nothing. It just is.'

'Aha.'

Aha what? Now I was getting confused. Maybe she was just messing with my head like she did with Clare about commitment. Why is she looking at me in that way? I ran the question through my mind again. Her eyes were on me daring me to continue. I dared not.

'Okay Gill, let me put it this way. A woman is an amazing sexual being with a thirst that can only be quenched by another woman. So being with a woman is like eating a mango. Something you do slowly, something you nibble at, so the juice just runs...'

No no no no. Don't ruin the fruit. No! Deep breathes Jilly. Deep breathes.

'No. Don't say another word!'

'You asked?'

The sparkle in her eye confirmed I had got the punishment I deserved. Her smile broadened. My understanding didn't.

'There is no need to discuss your sex life so why would I discuss mine?'

Even though the smile remained, I felt scolded. The

creamy liquid was cold, I drank it anyway. A small way to hide my discomfort.

'So, would you like to start the morning again with a proper conversation?'

It struck me at this point that even though all three of my closest friends were lesbians, I knew very little about that side of their lives. They always were so it always was. My curiosity was only piqued now because my mother was arriving in three hours and I wanted to present as a good lesbian. A good lesbian? Is there such a thing? I wasn't sure, and I definitely wasn't going to get the answers from Tex.

Travelling to the airport that morning I realised how much faith I had put into my friends. This charade would not be possible without them. Especially Tex. It was a scary situation for all. Tex had dressed no differently to normal even when I grumbled loudly. Tex just smiled and said, 'Yes lover.' Which infuriated me even more. In general, the trip to the airport was a quiet one except when I tried offering advice to Tex. Trivial things like 'I'm allergic to coconut' or 'we'd been on and off for years.' Tex would just nod and look out the window, frequently using her favourite phrase. A guarantee to place the car in silence for another five minutes. Just breathe.

'Mum!'

It was a relief to be out of Tex's company, even for a second.

'Gillian. Have you been eating?' As was customary she held me at arm's length. 'You look skinnier than normal.'

The scent of her perfume was strong, as I remembered

it to be. I wondered if all mums had their own fragrance. In years to come that smell would always make me think of her. She wore her Sunday bests partly because she would have been to church this morning and partly because she had come to the big smoke, the city. My mother was not what you'd call a petite woman. Father had always called her shapely. After the hours she spent labouring on the farm I'm not surprised. Plus, she always gave great hugs even if they were a little firm at times.

I imagined her telling her friends about going to the city to save her poor daughter from a childless life. She would have left out the gay part, but the trip was a mercy rescue. The women in her Country Women's Group would have fussed and offered friendly suggestions. That or offered sons, nephews or geeky bachelors.

As a child I would sit at her feet in the hair salon, while her hair was being set. The women would discuss all the goings on in the town. Little nods and winks would cover any lewd misdemeanour done by someone outside this circle. When you're small you don't take much notice of such goings on, now that I'm older, I realised I would have become part of that ritual. Not in my presence, more in my lack of it, and my lack of whatever else they deemed important. Namely a husband and children. The hug I gave my mother was full of resentment.

'You remember Tex Colbert don't you mum?'

I grimaced in anticipation, surprisingly they were very polite to each other.

'Tex Colbert. That's an unusual name dear.'

Mum recalled Tex from my graduation and various adventures I had described. The tamer ones at that. Finally, with mother collected and loaded, the three of us headed off to Harry and Clare's place.

Clare was very welcoming and chipper. The ever-reliable Clare I thought. She would have spent the morning cleaning her house and preparing food, the welcoming hostess. I definitely owe her one even if she claimed I didn't.

'Welcome everyone, come in. Nice to see you again Mrs Delene. Mr Delene not come with you?' Turning to allow us in the door, Clare bowed her head slightly.

'No dear, he has a showing this week-end.'

'Art?' Asked Tex.

'Oh no dear.' Chuckled mother. 'His Welsh Cardigan corgi, Charles, has a very important dog show to attend. Hopefully this'll be the one that makes him a champion.'

'Excellent!' Tex winked at me. 'Then you could stud him out?'

'No. Charlie wouldn't have the faintest what to do there. Too pampered and a little vague. Takes after Mr Delene you see.'

Mother's face had remained passive through the whole sentence. Mine had not though.

'Excellent!' Stated Tex once again.

'How about we move to the back deck.' Prompted Clare. She appeared to be moving us through the house as if staying too long inside was bad in some way.

'Can I get anyone a drink?'

I had known Clare a long time, she was hiding something in her voice. Looking at her face I saw a purplish bruise on one cheek. It looked recent, and painful. Smiling she waved me off when I was about to ask.

'Drinks?'

'Allow me.' Tex interrupted, leaning towards my mother. 'Mrs Delene?'

'Water will do fine.'

'Come on, something a little stronger. You don't seem a water gal to me.'

Mother doesn't drink were the words coming to mind when Tex prompted.

'Well maybe a little scotch on the rocks. That would be lovely dear.'

My mouth must have fallen open.

'You catching fly's Gillian? Now your mother didn't teach you to stand agape like that.'

My second scolding for the day and it wasn't even 11 am.

'And you my love?'

It took a few seconds to realise Tex was referring to me. To me! I gave her my harshest eyes before responding.

'Just the normal.' I smiled sweetly too. Let her work that one out.

Clare moved this happy little party out to the deck where finger foods were already laid out. As she went to fetch Harry, she mumbled something about a damn computer. It nearly sounded like she swore which was not like her, she moved so fast I missed most of it. I made a note to ask her about the bruise later, when we were alone.

'Here you are Mrs Delene.' The crystal glass Tex handed mother sloshed with liquid.

'My that is a large one,' she surmised, but as Tex offered to make another, mother declined. 'That would be wasteful, dear.'

Tex had the audacity to sit on the arm of my chair as she offered my drink.

'And for you my love.'

I took a sip from the tall glass and was shocked to discover it was my usual. A tall cranberry juice with a slice of lemon and a shot of vodka. I sat stunned as Tex smiled and slid an arm behind my back.

'So, Mrs Delene, what are your plans while you are here?'

Tex probably asked so she would know how long she had to suffer. It was most certainly a question on my agenda.

'Just some shopping and sightseeing. And, of course, some quality time with my daughter.'

I'm sure my mother's smile was forced. I think I'm becoming paranoid. Come now Gillian, Tex is just playing the part. I should be thankful.

'I have some time off if you'd like me to show you around.'

Tex! Deep frigging breaths Jilly.

Harry came down and greeted us all. Thank goodness, my heart was palpitating. Strangely Clare nearly looked more nervous than me. That was until mother asked Tex what she did for a living. Then we all looked nervous. Me mostly. Please God, I promise to donate more to charities and be a better Christian. Please.

'I'm a photographer.'

'Ooo. What sort dear?'

Please God, anything. Anything you ask. Tex leant towards mother; her head was at my height just forward a little. What was that brain thinking? I was going to die. I know it.

'More drinks.' Interrupted Clare. I love Clare.

'I take portraiture shots. Mainly of pretty women, none are as beautiful as my Jilly.'

Nooooooooooo. Well God, take me now. Hang on, that wasn't too bad. Was it? Harry's baritone laugh bubbled to the surface before quickly changing to a cough. Clare let out a breath she wasn't aware she was holding and Tex in turn gave me a wink and a quick hug. I'm sure I turned into vapour that very moment. If only the wind would carry me away.

'Marvellous. Maybe you could take a few shots of Charles. I could pay you of course.'

'I'd absolutely love to. On one condition. I never charge family.'

Tex sipped her beer casually. Her arm was the only thing holding me upright in the chair. My mind quickly returned to this morning's conversation over the creamy coffee. Ground rules. That is what we should have discussed. A contract even. Like all contracts, one must specify the terms or else the other party has free range. Obviously, in this situation I did not look further than the image of dating Tex. Tonight. Yes, tonight we would discuss the ground rules.

~ 4 ~

Tex and mother hit it off spectacularly. It was a void whether mother would act well to such a thing or not because she had met very few of my partners before, and none of them had been female. Maybe it was because Tex kept refilling mother's glass, or because she was a country girl at heart, something tugged at my mother's heartstrings. In turn, I felt a great weight lift from my shoulders. Mother's visit, I decided, was going to pass peacefully.

'She's pretty cool your Mum.'

I sensed some admiration. I watched Tex's reflection as I brushed my teeth. The bathroom door framed her body. She leant there casually watching me.

'Yeah. I suppose she is.'

Pride filled my chest, I was surprised. Slipping past Tex, I was also surprised to see mother in our room. Her nightie was on backwards, and I could smell the scotch on her from my side of the room.

'Mum?'

'Just wanted to say goodnight.'

A sloppy kiss landed on my forehead. Tex laughed till one landed on her too.

'Night mum.'

'Night Mrs Delene.' Wiping the saliva from her face, Tex moved towards the bed.

'Call me mum. Since you're part of the family now.'

Hey! What happened to the mother who didn't approve of sex before marriage? Here she was now, after only knowing Tex for one afternoon, adding her to the family.

Tex said 'okay' and looked to me for salvation. Leading mother by the shoulders I hustled her to the spare room and tucked the blankets tight about her. With a kiss to her forehead I made a mad dash back to my room. The look on Tex's face made me want to burst. Quickly I shut the door to muffle our laughter.

Already in bed Tex looked comfortable. She was propped up by some pillows, smiling sweetly at me. Looking down at the satin nightie I wore, I blushed. I hoped she didn't think I wore this on her account. I made a mental note to wear flannel tomorrow night. Sliding into the cool sheets, I placed an imaginary line between us, then decided to bring up my ground rules.

'Maybe before this goes too much further, we should set up some rules.'

'Rules?'

Her hand brushed a lock of hair from my eyes. I could feel the rosiness in my cheeks. Pulling the sheet to my neck I continued.

'Mum is to like you though not adore you.'

'Strange rule. Wouldn't her liking me help your cause?'

The way her head tilted made her look so innocent. Something I knew she wasn't.

'Well yes. And no.'

I think a little parcel of jealousy had swept over me this afternoon, fortunately it had passed.

'When I finally meet someone, I want her to adore them.'

'Aha. When you meet a man.'

Tex swirled her hat on the bedpost and leant in close. Way past a person's, well my own, personal boundary.

'Yes.' Her breath brushed my nose. It tickled making it twitch.

'And displays of affection.'

Curiosity piqued; her attention focused solely on me.

'Should be limited.'

'To what? Hand holding?'

Her hand embraced mine warmly.

'Nuzzling?'

As she drew closer towards my cheek, I could feel her breath brush against my face, the hairs on my neck pricked. Then Tex moved away from my cheek towards my ear. Oh god, not my ear! The tip of her nose circled my ear. Increasing, my heartbeat near punched a hole through my chest. Not my ear! Then I felt a nibble

'Kissing?'

I drew back. My facial expression must have been of pure terror as Tex broke into hysterical laughter. Disgusted I rolled over, separating us with my back. Laughter continued to assault me, and it continued for what seemed an eternity. I pretended to be asleep when she asked me if there were any other rules?

Morning only broke the chain of horrendous dreams. My last was that I selected gay men to be my boyfriends.

We would sit in front of Judy Garland movies laughing or crying. Barbara Streisand would play in the background. And I would only figure out they were gay after months of dating with no sex. In the dream, each gay boyfriend would not leave and eventually I had a collection of about six hanging around. They kept asking me if I could not see the truth about who I picked. In the last phase of the dream they suggest I ask a woman out. In a busy coffee shop, I tap one on the shoulder to ask her out and who should it be? Tex! I awoke startled. Twisted tightly in the sheets, I realise, with relief that I am by myself. There is chatter downstairs, I assume mother and Tex, though for the moment I am happy to be alone.

'Good morning Gillian. Sleep well?'

Mother showed no ill effects from yesterday.

'I don't know, she tossed and turned a lot last night.'

There was a twinkle in those eyes.

'Coffee my love?'

Barely saying a word, I took the coffee and sat down. To my surprise Tex was just serving scrambled eggs and bacon. Devouring it hungrily, mother took seconds. I ate mine slowly while Tex just sipped black coffee. Peering over the mug's lip, Tex took in my mother.

'There's lots more there Mrs D ... Oops, mum.'

'She's a gem to have around dear.'

Mother winked at me. This was not my mother. Aliens must have taken her on that flight. That or I'm still dreaming. Maybe it was still Saturday and I'm fantasizing all of this before I ask Tex for her help? No. Tex just kicked me under the table, and it hurts.

~ 5 ~

Harry walked to the oven and drew the door open as she had done many times before. Even though it was warm the oven held only an empty plate. Switching the oven off, Harry moved towards the lounge room. A burnt smell lingered in the air.

'Clare!'

No response came.

'Clare, where are you?'

Harry walked along the hall. The lounge room dark as it was had been empty, as had the spare room. Continuing she approached the room that had become her home office. The pungent burnt smell grew stronger.

'What the hell?'

Harry's computer was shattered across the desk. A baseball bat hung precariously on the mangled mess. Nothing had been spared, even the printer lay in pieces. Glass from the screen was scattered everywhere, across the chair and on the floor.

'Clare are you okay?'

A sense of urgency flooded Harry, and panic, as she grabbed the bat. Her pulse quickened in anticipation. She did not know what to expect. Throwing the bedroom door open she was ready to tackle any intruder.

'Clare?'

The word came out as a near whisper. Her eyes scanned the room. The king bed poised in the middle looked undisturbed as did the side tables. To be honest it looked as per normal. Scanning the room, Harry made a mental count of the contents, hoping to reaffirm all was okay. The only thing even slightly out of place was a red overnight travel bag on the bed. Harry couldn't recall seeing that particular bag before and wondered if a burglar was still in the house and whether this was their stash bag.

'Oh, your home.'

Clare was calm as she appeared from the ensuite. With bat poised to strike, Harry was caught by surprise. She tried to hold her voice steady as she didn't want Clare to see how unsettled she felt. As a precaution she looked beyond Clare into the ensuite just to make sure no-one was hiding there.

'What happened?'

Harry moved towards Clare, one hand lowering the bat, the other coming to rest on Clare's shoulder.

'Nothing.'

Clare brushed Harry's hand aside while continuing to carry some personal items to the bed. Several toiletries were balancing precariously in her hands. She dumped them into the red bag.

Grabbing her roughly, Harry dragged Clare to face her.

'Let me go Harry.'

'What the hell are you doing?'

'Me? What the hell have you been doing Harry?' Clare was over it. Over the arguments, over the aggression, over the untruths that Harry continued to sprout.

'Don't be smart with me. What about my computer!?'

Spittle formed in the corners of Harry's mouth. Her unsteadiness replaced with anger. Harry slammed the bat down on the dresser dislodging the mirror it held. Crashing to the floor it disintegrated into a million tiny pieces.

'There's your answer to everything.'

'My answer? I would have preferred to hit something else. You broke my fucking computer, Clare.'

'And you've been cheating on me, Harry. Seems fair.'

'What?'

'Oh, don't deny it, that only embarrasses you and me. The only question left is how long?'

'How long?'

'Yes, how long have I been an idiot. How long have I been married to a cheater, a liar, a worthless piece of crap!'

Clare's voice had risen above anything Harry had ever heard before. This was frightening. Harry felt like a wild animal cornered. What was the right answer?

'I'm sorry. We can get through this.'

'Really? You think this is fixable?'

'Don't throw what we have built together away. Look what we have?'

'I have a cheating partner. What do you have?'

'Look Clare.' In her anger Harry grabs Clare's arm and roughly turns her towards herself. 'This is fixable.'

Tugging herself free Clare comes within inches of Harry's face. Nose to nose.

'That will be the last time you will ever, ever, touch me.' Forceful emphasis was placed on the second ever.

Clare was unsure whether that was to reinforce the point to herself or to Harry.

For the briefest moment both contemplate what just happened. Clare realizes that more than a mirror lay on the floor between them, irretrievable and shattered. There was only one thing to do.

'This can't be fixed Harry.'

Clare zipped the red bag, swung it over her shoulder and left. She left without a second glance back. She wouldn't have seen through the tears anyway.

~ 6 ~

Before this adventure Tex had only heard biased stories of my mother. It dawned on me; I only informed my friends of the grief my mother caused. It hadn't crossed my mind to tell of the special things only mothers do. This trip allowed me to see my mother in a new light.

With work so hectic there was no way I could escape and enjoy my mother's company as much as I'd have liked. Tentatively I allowed Tex to show her around town. I couldn't believe how well she and my mother were getting along. During the daylight hours they did the touristy thing and shopped. Tex the perfect host. At night they would regale their stories of the day's events. One time someone had mistaken them for lovers. I was speechless to say the least. And a little jealous, not of the lover thing more of the time spent just being ... happy.

'So mum, having a nice trip?'

We were lounging one evening in front of the television. Tex had popped out and for the first time in two days I had my mother to myself. It brought mixed emotions.

'Why yes Gillian. The most fun I've had in a while. Tex and I visited the valley. And she took me into some extraordinary shops.'

Laughter bubbled from her in a steady flow as she remembered the day's outing. Something I was not involved in. I partially hoped she would expand on the story, a small part of me hoped she wouldn't.

'If only I didn't have to work tomorrow.'

'It's okay Gillian; I think Tex has made plans to keep me busy. She really is a nice girl.'

A nice girl. Yes mother, if only you knew. The type that enjoys looking for a win on a Friday night. Or any other night for that matter.

'Yes, I think so.'

Did my smile look sincere? I don't think she even looked up from the television to notice. I refocus my attention on the television and the room falls quiet. My mind is not. One person's dream had become my nightmare. My make-believe partner and my mother got along. How could they? Weren't mother-in-law's the bane of the earth? Their existence so painful that in India they have mother-in-law prisons, locking the nuisance away.

Next day.

'You look preoccupied Jilly.'

'JoJo, I didn't expect Tex and Mother to get along so well.'

I continued to wipe the bench as we spoke. It now seemed a ritual we performed more than a sense of cleaning. Though it may be JoJo's way of ensuring a quality clean.

'Today they are going to the beach. Can you imagine Tex with all those bikini laden women and my mother?'

My mother, a woman in her fifties! JoJo just smirked and rang the service bell. I snatched the plate, checked the ticket and stomped from the kitchen. A small smile rose upon my face as I considered Tex and my mother at the beach.

'Hey Clare, I didn't know you were in today.'

I lay the plate before my friend and arranged her silverware.

'Meeting up with Harry?'

'No.'

'So, what happened to your eye?' The bruising still looked painful.

'It's nothing Jilly.'

'Really? It looks more painful than nothing.'

A small pause followed before Clare continued.

'You know, one of those night-time mishaps.'

'Yeah, had my share of clumsy moments.'

More than my share. My life was a whole clumsy moment. I was about to return to the kitchen yet hesitated.

'I want to thank you for the brunch the other day. Mother had a wonderful time.' The memory of my discomfort sent a small shiver up my spine.

'Anything to help a friend.'

Clare smiled at me, her eyes didn't sparkle as they normally did. She seemed sadder, I wondered if that was just wincing due to the pain of her eye.

'You sure you're okay Clare? You seem, well I don't know, flatter than normal.'

'Just tired, you know. How are you and Tex getting along?'

'Surprisingly well.'

We both chuckled together. The murmur of happiness

faded and for the briefest moment I sensed an awkward silence.

'Are you really okay Clare?'

'Yeah I'll survive. You know me.'

Clare gave me that smile once again. I sensed a need to talk more, the little bell rang demanding my attention. Instead of staying I scurried off to the kitchen. It was just before the lunch rush, though it was busy enough to stop me from returning to Clare as quickly as I would have liked. From across the room I could see her deep in thought. She had barely touched her meal by the time I returned.

'Not hungry?' I appeared to have startled her.

'Not much.'

It was then that I noticed her hands torturing a small brochure.

'Domestic violence? You thinking of taking it up?'

I had managed to draw a smile. Thankfully she must have thought it as ludicrous as I did. Her and Harry, domestic violence, pfft.

'No.'

She looked at me as if she wished to say something but stopped.

'One of your clients?' I asked, considering the gay youth helpline Clare had volunteered with for the past six years.

'Yeah. Look Jilly I may have to go away for a little while for work. I'll be out of contact. Could you watch over Harry for me? Make sure she's, well, okay?' Clare's voice faded.

'Sure Clare. Definitely. Besides I think Harry will be fine and will cope without you.' I'd never seen them take a day apart. So, I added not very convincingly. 'At least for a short while.'

'Thanks.'

Clare rose, and with a hug as a good-bye she handed me the payment for her meal and left. That was the last I saw of her though I didn't recall this conversation till much later. Actually, I was too pre-occupied with my own little home-grown dilemmas.

Mother is gone and my house was my own again.

'Your mum is really cool.'

Tex said while she relaxed in our bed. Her lanky frame settled into a comfortable groove.

'Yeah it was sad to see her go. I wish I had spent more time with her. To be honest I was a little jealous of the time you spent with her.'

'Don't be. All she talked about was you.'

Tex flashed the briefest smile before rolling over and snuggling in for the night. I too rolled over, comfortable and relaxed. As sleep weighted my eyes to a point of no return, I wondered why Tex was still in my bed. More to the point, why was she still in my house, especially since mother had flown out that day. This final thought was lost in a flurry of unremarkable dreams.

~ 7 ~

The rain pattered on the bus window drumming a never-ending rhythm into Clare's head. In some obscure way, it matched the hum of the tyres and the squelch of the wipers. Clare's head was already about to explode, and this added commotion was not helping. Fortunately, her stop was next.

Departing the bus alone Clare found herself on a vacant block with the sound of the ocean just audible beyond the rain, beyond the darkness of the night. Once the rear red lights of the bus disappear around the bend, she finds herself completely alone. Clare had been here in happier times, and sunnier times. Heavy rain saturated her hair which now falls limply to her shoulders. On occasion, several strands lead a torrent of water down her face. Pushing them aside, Clare feels the torrent glide down some other part of her head.

As she waits the rain starts to settle though the clouds remain, holding the world in darkness. Occasional flashes of lightning illuminate the world around her. Turning towards the vacant block she walks up the rise, the sound of waves crashing on rocks as her guide. After another flash of light, she sees a small post with a white tip indicating a possible path. Without hesitating she follows the overgrown path as if it were a popular thoroughfare, pausing often to wait for lightning to reveal it further.

Her shoes, fully sodden, fumble over the loose sand and gravel. Hands outstretched; Clare runs her fingertips over the long grass as if she was running through a field on a sunny day. Grass tips tenderly bow to her touch. In the distance, Clare can see the silhouette of a tree. Behind it, the emerging moon glows through a hazy sheet of receding rain, making it look magical. The mystical silhouette being her destination.

After stumbling a little more Clare finally reaches the tree. The trunk is rough under her touch. Its thick roots protrude from the dirt, threatening to trip unsuspecting visitors. Touching the trunk knowingly, Clare uses it as a guide to the cliff edge. Clinging tightly to the tree she peers over the edge of the cliff. At that moment, a huge wave crashes against the rocks below, sending a salty spray skywards to where Clare stands.

Licking her lips she laughs. Leaning further she waits for the next salty saturation. To heighten the thrill, Clare releases the grasp of one hand from the tree. She stands dangling over the cliff face in expectation. The jagged rocks below look somehow inviting. Clare is enjoying the view of the moon speckled rocks when suddenly, the next salty wave, catches her by surprise.

My life absorbed me so much that I had no idea what my dearest friend was up to. We all have paths to take and lives to live.

At first, I didn't realise, as it took a while before it dawned on me, my mother's visit had shifted the axis of my world slightly. Now what was I to do? Tex was still sleeping in my bed and my mother left seven days ago! How do you approach such a subject?

One evening as we settled on the lounge to watch our favourite movie, The Proposal, I attempted to broach the subject.

'Tex.'

'Yeah.' Tex responded, her eyes remained glued to the television. Sitting right next to me, her hand randomly dived into the bowl of popcorn on my lap.

'You haven't gone out much lately. Surely it must be boring staying in each night with me?' And restricting your lifestyle by living in my house.

'Surprisingly no.' Her gaze stayed fixed on the television.

'Oh.'

Oh? Surely that's not the appropriate response. Oh. I sat quietly, my hand lingering over the popcorn. What words were I looking for? Get out? Hmm appropriate I suppose. I hadn't felt this awkward about a question since mum's very English, and very white, hairdresser gave birth to an ethnic baby when I was ten. Especially since her husband was also very English and very white. Pigmentation I was told. Was Tex now an unremovable blotch on my life? My thoughts were suddenly disrupted.

'Hey lover, I'm going to bed now. You need anything?'

Tex rested her hand on my shoulder as she rounded the lounge. She seemed, what was the word? Sincere? Well yes Tex, I need you to leave my house! All I could mumble though was a no. I followed shortly after. I suppose if

I wanted to make a point, I could have slept in the guest room. I was going to try one night, then Tex bailed me up to show me an article in a magazine. One of those men's magazines to be exact. The article was interesting, and we sat in bed discussing it for a few hours. By the time Tex turned the light out I realised I had failed in my mission. Besides, this is my house and my bed, why should I have to move out of it.

JoJo laughed as I reported my dilemma.

'So, let me get this straight. You wished for this to be convincing and now that it is you are unhappy.'

'Yes. Well no.'

JoJo always twisted my words. As usual, my nervous energy had me scrubbing a bench. I'm sure JoJo entertained these discussions just to have brilliantly clean benches.

'Why are you so scared to ask her to leave? I would have thrown that hussy out the moment your mother left. Straight from the car honey.'

JoJo's face contorted into a wry smile.

'Why should I have to ask? She just should.'

'Are you enjoying her company?'

'Well yes, that doesn't mean a thing.' Surely.

'Is she a bad housemate?'

As he spoke JoJo started carving an apple. Somehow, he seemed to take more care and time considering the apple's outcome than my own dilemma. I hate that apple.

'Not at all. Most nights she has dinner on the table waiting for me. And she picks up after herself. That's not the point.'

Surely just because someone is easy to live with doesn't

mean you should. With the twist of his hand JoJo had made that stupid apple into a swan. I'm starting to wonder if JoJo knows how to make anything else other than swans. And whether swans were actually useful.

'Admit it you like having someone there. A warm body is way better than a cold bed.'

True in a sense. The essence of loneliness had vanished since Tex was around. If I was to still look for that somebody special how was I to explain the situation. I can see it now, me taking someone home, whisking them to my bedroom and saying don't mind her she's my make-believe girlfriend. Hmmm, the fact is I can't see me meeting anyone, let alone whisking them to my bedroom. Was Tex really the closest thing I'd ever get to marriage? Wow.

Talking about marriage I hadn't seen Clare in two weeks. I rang Harry a couple of times, she seemed down, I thought it was because the love of her life was away. She protested that she was fine, was working hard and didn't need to go for drinks.

'Come on Harry. How about dinner at my house with me and Tex.'

There was no laughter about the line 'me and Tex'. This surprised me more than anything. There was no response to it at all. How unusual.

'No. Thanks Jilly. I have work.' A sadness was evident in her voice. 'Have you heard from her?'

'No, I was just about to ask you that. Where did she go again?'

Come to think of it I was so fixated on my life I had

forgotten the most obvious question, again. How good a friend could I be I wondered?

'Away.'

Harry barely uttered another word though she did allow me to prattle for a short while, then she was gone. Something about a printer error or something.

Wow, I suddenly couldn't think what my life would be like without Tex. Should I be scared? Possibly not, though the sight I got when I arrived home scared me a little. Tex had clothes scattered all about our bed, I mean my bed. Before I could utter a word, her voice went into rapid talk mode.

'Your mum rang. She's invited us to visit. Isn't that exciting? Apparently, Charles will officially be crowned a champion this week-end and your dad wants all the family there to celebrate.'

'Mum rang?' One question out of the hundreds in my head. 'All the family?' Was the next prominent one.

'It's only Wednesday so I figured we could drive up starting tomorrow. Planes really aren't my thing. We could have an overnight in Bundaberg and be in Rocky by Friday afternoon. Then it's just a short hop out to your parents. I've programmed the GPS already. Though we will have to make a small detour in the morning. Your mum wants me to pick something up for her.'

Tex's eyes were wide with excitement, like a child at Christmas. I'd never seen her this way before.

'I have work.'

The protest was a mixture of confusion and relief.

'All taken care of. I rang JoJo. He was very concerned

that you had been working too hard of late. He said take a couple of weeks off. He seemed nicer than I remembered him to be.'

'You have to work.'

I blurt the next obvious excuse.

'Nope. I'm owed a tonne of time off plus they've asked me to do a story on it for one of their other magazines, A Dog's Life or something. I've always wanted to write.'

Really? Tex write? I wasn't even sure if she was literate.

~ 8 ~

'Clare. It's me Harry, again. I miss you. I really wish you'd take my call. Voice messages are so ... impersonal. I miss your voice. I miss your touch. I miss your smell on my clothes.'

Harry interjects with a small laugh.

'I even miss you being right all the time. You were right about me the first time we spoke. I was a nobody heading nowhere. You should have listened to your own advice.'

The line falls into silence as Harry bites her lower lip.

'The only reason I succeeded at anything was so that I wouldn't be a failure in your eyes. And in a way, so that I could, or at least attempt to be, good enough for you. You are my world, I know that words alone will not bring you back. I have failed you. I have become someone I hate. An unknown in my own skin.'

Some words arrive quickly while others hold back. Harry attempts to make sense of them so they would make sense to Clare. Holding back tears Harry looks for the right words, the words that would bring Clare back.

'My anger was not aimed at you, though you received the blows. I was angry for myself. For being lost. For not being me. I should have spoken to you about it. How I was feeling. Instead I was a coward and blamed you for my failure. You have been the only shining star in my life.'

The tears flow more steadily now.

'I had a shit life growing up. You were my only salvation. The only one who saw me as I was, and what I could be. Who loved me for being me. I suppose after fifteen years I had taken that for granted. I had taken you for granted. Forgive me. Honestly if I was you, I would never forgive me. Please let me know that you are ok. Send me a text. Or contact Jilly.'

In the pit of her stomach Harry fears the worse. The words for this fear do not surface, instead she begs Clare to make contact; any contact.

'I love you Clare, and I truly am sorry. I'm seeing a counsellor. I'm trying to be better. I know, I should have done it earlier. I pray it's not too late for us. Can you see it in your heart to forgive me? Set any terms you want, and I will meet them.'

It was Harry's final desperate plea. Harry was drained. The voicemail was full. A stark beep was the end of the conversation.

~ 9 ~

Mother's pre-trip pick-up request now had me waiting in the car at the far end of the valley mall. From here I could see the garish neon green flicker from a sign at one of the clubs. It was sort of like a frog, with purple neon bursting from its head. Instantly I knew it was the Horny Toad, a club I was often dragged to by my friends.

The pedestrian mall was busier than I expected. As Chinatown was a parallel pedestrian mall one line of buildings away, I assumed many were here for lunch. Possibly yum cha. It made me kind of hungry thinking of all those tasty steamed treats like dumplings, rice noodles and pork buns. Once on a dare I tried steamed chicken feet. Not something I'd recommend.

Tex had been gone for several minutes. The night before had passed in a blur of packing and confusion in regard to Tex's excitement of going to my parent's. Hell, I hadn't made the trip for two years now. It was never on my 'to do' list, so why was it on hers? As part of a perverse game of torture?

Tex came bounding along the paved mall. Her boots jingling as onlookers turned curiously towards the sound. How can one woman attract so much attention? Then again, how could one woman, such as myself, attract so little. Sigh. Tex had her broadest smile as she hopped in the car.

'Let's go.'

'What's in the paper bag?'

My curiosity had been aroused last night. Tex wasn't revealing any information.

'You'll have to ask your mother.'

Tex smirked then looked straight ahead through the windscreen.

'Let's go.'

I moved off in the direction indicated by the GPS.

'Do we really need this?'

The GPS, which Tex had christened Gertie, was now telling me where to turn in a not so soothing voice.

'Your mum thought you may have forgotten the way.'

First, I have a mother who nags me about not coming home enough and now I have a ... Hmmm, what is Tex classed as? She's not really make-believe, she's not really real. Partner real I mean. This was worth some pondering.

Luckily, I have close to four hundred kilometres to ponder this before our overnight stop at Bundaberg. Surprisingly Tex had, since yesterday afternoon, time to research sights of interest on the way. However, did she manage that? I barely remembered my toothbrush.

'So, lover.'

The word still left her mouth in a breathy manner. It apparently still amused her greatly as she grinned like the Cheshire cat as she turned to face me.

'Looking forward to going home?'

Her camera was raised, pointed in my direction. The

shutter fluttered in the lens as she clicked the button. Lover. Lover! How could she call me that since we have never done IT. Not even close, however she still persisted in calling me this name after my mother left. I hadn't done it with anyone for longer than I care to remember. Oh my gosh. In some perverse way did Tex enjoy torturing me or was it an act of kindness? Kindness from Tex, I doubt it.

'Do you have to call me that?'

My focus on the road was distracted by her. I didn't ask in an aggravated way, more in a resigned disappointment with myself.

'Still avoiding the question Gill?'

Her non-chalantness was starting to drive me crazy.

'Sure, I'm happy to go home.'

Like the prodigal daughter returning home.

'Then how come you haven't been in two years?'

What? Did she and my mother make a pact to gang up on me? Play on my childhood guilt? Why should I return home to a place where my father, who I might add always wanted a son, prefers his pet corgi over human companionship? Home, a place where my mother has an inalienable way of pinpointing all of my insecurities, and weaknesses, and is keen to highlight them each time we talk.

'Hang on Gill.'

Hang on? Hang on to what? I was so preoccupied in my own thoughts I didn't hear the booby song as Tex's phone rang. How insulting a song, I thought. Who Would knowingly put that in their phone? Then use it?

'Yep, got it. And I got the colour you wanted.'

She told the person at the other end of the line.

'No, no, we will be there tomorrow afternoon. Love you too!'

With that Tex hung up.

'Was that my mother?'

MY mother may I highlight.

'Yeah, I told mum we had picked up her parcel.'

'In the colour she wanted?'

Tex appeared pleased with herself.

'Yes. I told her we'd be on time tomorrow.'

'Did she want to speak to me?'

Or could I at least have the option to speak to MY mother.

'No, she was in a hurry, she was on her mobile. She just wanted to check on the parcel.'

The parcel. The damn parcel. Since when were you and my mother on phone terms? Since when did you exchange mobile numbers? My mother has a mobile phone? The road in front of me blurred slightly. Was I even relevant on this trip? Black speckles distorted my view further. Was I even relevant? At all?

'Gill!'

The crude version of my name startled me. I hit the brakes just in time to miss a broken-down caravan. The car swerved onto the loose roadside gravel before the Jeep pulled to a halt just centimetres from a huge gum tree.

'Jeez. You okay Jilly?'

'Yeah. Yeah, I just lost concentration.'

Tex's concern appeared real. Exiting the car she ran to my door and swung it open. Releasing the tension, it previously held, my body sagged into the seat further. My head fell back onto the headrest. Tex had snatched the keys from the ignition all the while turning to apologise to the old couple whose caravan had nearly been wiped out by a lunatic. Namely me.

'You appeared to blank out there.'

Tex placed her warm palm on my forehead. I didn't move so her palms were placed onto a cheek each and slowly turned my face to hers.

'You okay?'

I barely managed to push her away as my seat belt caught my forward falling body. There I hung half in and half out of the car with my stomach contents pouring from my mouth. Wisely Tex washed me up and placed me into the passenger side of the vehicle, but not before she took a few happy snaps of the location for prosperity's sake. Surely, pictures of irate caravaners and roadside gravel would have no value to anyone. The rest of the drive to Bundaberg passed in a blur.

~ 10 ~

Harry snatched the mobile up on its first ring. Looking at the familiar number her heart leapt.

'Clare!'

'Sorry no. This is Sergeant Beilby from the Noosa Heads police.'

Noosa Heads police. Harry was confused. It took a few moments for the possibilities to sink in.

'We have retrieved this phone and this number was the emergency contact.'

'Emergency contact?'

'Yes. I'm looking for a Harry?'

'That's me. Harry, I mean Harriette, Harriette Granger, Harry for short. What's happened to Clare?'

Every worst-case scenario was running through Harry's mind. Kidnapping. Car crash. Murder.

'Ms Granger may I ask your relationship to Clare?'

His voice was official, unemotional.

'She's my wife! I mean partner.' I mean the love of my life, the sole reason for my existence thought Harry. 'Where is she?'

'Clare's whereabouts is currently unknown to us.'

The officer paused, attempting to word the next section correctly.

'We have found this mobile, a small handbag and a gold ring. They were found near a tree.'

'A tree?' Her wedding band was found near a tree. Harry felt empty.

'Yes, a tree on a cliff face at Hell's Gate in the Noosa Heads Reserve. We have concerns for her safety.'

'As in falling? No then the items wouldn't be near the tree, would they? Then do you mean ... suicide?'

'We aren't making speculations here we are just looking at facts.'

Facts thought Harry. Fact one: Clare's personal items were in a tree. Fact two: this tree was on a cliff. Fact three: no one has heard from Clare for over a week. The shocking thought was that not much speculation was needed.

'When was the last time you saw her?'

'Eight days ago, I think. She left for a while.' It was a teary held back whisper.

'Left?' Enquired the officer.

Harry imagined the notes he was jotting down. Namely how did a partner not notice when the love of their life doesn't come home. For weeks. It sort of makes them look guilty. Harry felt guilty, not in the way the officer may be thinking, although guilty all the same. She was also feeling utterly distraught.

'Your partner left eight days ago.' It was more a statement than a question. 'Have you had contact with her since then?'

'No.'

The ever so organised Tex had pre-booked us into a quaint motel in a leafy part of Bundaberg. Leafy was not going to remove my sombre mood. All I wanted was a nice shower and a quiet lay down. The drive had been interesting, probably more so if you were ten. We had paused at the Big Pineapple in Nambour for an ice cream Sunday and to take some photos of the oversized fibreglass fruit. The sixteen metre high pineapple set on acres and acres of pineapple plants was truly stunning. Tex made me stand at the yellow base for a picture then I had to climb the stairs to the artificial leafy top for another. That was morning tea. All I remember was fields and fields of sugar cane and pineapple plants.

It was a standard style of motel consisting of a long line of single level rooms with car spaces a mere step or two from the door. Some rooms had garden chairs which I suppose was for smokers. Our room had nothing other than a sad looking pot plant out the front. The room itself had an overwhelming fresh smell, with a heavy hint of eucalyptus disinfectant, that initially took my breath away, and brought back my nausea. I'm guessing the staff were probably trying to cover up that strange musty smell that lingered behind the freshness. The small space also had a built in bench, hiding a mini fridge, and space on top for the kettle and complimentary tea and coffee. Hey, they even had complimentary biscuits.

With my head still dizzy I made my way to the shower while Tex unpacked the car. The steam ran up my nostrils making my head feel clearer. The water pounded my body, massaging it into a better shape, or at least I hoped so. The heat engulfed me making me feel warm and secure thus lifting my mood.

I'd been in such a hurry to enter the shower that as I turned the taps off, I realised I hadn't brought any clothes into the bathroom with me. Fortunately, there was a pile of folded towels nearby. I roughly dried myself with one and wrapped it about my body. Damn motels, always skimping on costs, the towel barely wrapped around me. A hand was urgently required to keep it up. The second towel was used to secure my damp hair high on my head.

You know, not much thought was put into the next moment. Here I was a towel wrapped around my head like a turban. My hands frantically attempting to hold, a too small towel, about my body. I've always been modest even when I was alone in my own house.

Stepping through the bathroom door I was caught by surprise. Tex lay calmly on the queen bed, her hat tilted slightly over her eyes as if she were asleep. If only. In that moment she smiled and threw me a soda. Instinct is a sucky thing. I released my grasp on the towel to catch the can. With no support the towel quickly fell to the floor. The can was colder than expected and as my fingers fumbled with it, I managed to drop it on my toe.

Once again instinct kicked in. Completely forgetting

about the lost towel, I grabbed my throbbing toe. Hopping on the spot, cursing Tex, I managed to trip on the dropped towel thus landing completely naked on the bed next to Tex. My once neat turban had fallen to cover my head completely. A sense of claustrophobia kicked in. I wrestled with the towel until I was able to untangle myself and throw it across the room. With a deep sigh I let my body relax.

The background laughter which I apparently had managed to block out was replaced with a wolf whistle. My mind screamed at me not to, still, I turned my head to see Tex whose body was now running parallel facing mine. Her head resting on her palm, her elbow supporting her body so that it was just raised above mine. Cockily she flicked her hat back. The only thing I was grateful for was that her camera wasn't at hand.

'What a floor show. Women have been known to leap into bed with me, but I've gotta say that was the most awesome attempt ever.'

Aarrrgh. What more was there to say? I snatched at the bed covers, her weight pinned them down. Her eyes challenged me. I didn't respond. I didn't move. I didn't do anything. With a sigh Tex rose.

'Okay. I'll grab a quick shower while you get ready.'

'Ready for what?'

I was looking forward to a quiet night in. Then again that would be more time spent with Tex .... alone. Surely 400 kilometres was enough time together.

'Why don't you go out and I'll stay in.'

A laugh was my answer. In that briefest sound she had

challenged me again. I knew there was no way she would let me 'stay in'.

Her plan was simple, a tour of the Bundaberg Rum Distillery, followed by a few samplers, then possibly dinner somewhere. Didn't sound that tortuous I suppose, except that her pesky camera was coming along.

The tour was actually quite interesting. It all started where the trains brought the cane in from the numerous farms. Mid way we were surrounded by the largest stainless-steel vats. Some with a sloshing sound inside. The brewing of rum from sugar cane has a rather delicious pungent smell. Tex jingled through the tour with a smug look on her face. At times she grabbed my elbow to guide me. Each time I snatched my arm back.

'Come now lover.'

She would whisper. I'm convinced my life is a game to her. I was just wondering when she'd get tired of me.

The tour ended with the small group encircled around a large wooden bar. Here we managed to taste the many brews of the distillery. I've never had rum before so this was a new experience for me. Tex threw them back as if they were soda.

In fact, Tex had a line of drinks before her. Some from the other patrons, and a few from the girl behind the bar. Unexpectedly Tex laughed loudly as the girl lent in and whispered something in her ear. Tex raised her glass to the girl and smiled. That lopsided kind of smile. I wonder if that added to her supposed appeal or whether the girl didn't notice.

Me? I sat a stool away cradling an empty glass.

'Here Gill have a few of these, I'll never get through them all.'

Was her smile sympathetic? Or did I just look pathetic. My head was light from the day. I was hoping the feeling would go away, it didn't so I decided to drink it away. Probably not the wisest move for a one pot screamer. Before I knew it, the night had vanished and Tex had me propped against our motel door.

'Come lover. Time you were in bed.'

Why does she always smile that lopsided smile at me? Is it meant to be mocking or endearing, I can never tell?

'Why do you call me lover? We've never slept together?'

Whoa. My thoughts actually exited my mouth. How unusual. Her laugh wrapped around me.

'We sleep together all the time.'

The door swung open and I stumbled into the room. It was spinning so fiercely I had to grab onto the wall.

'No, no. We have never done it.'

The words tumbled from my mouth in a slur.

'It?'

For some strange reason I grabbed Tex's vest with my two hands and dragged her to me.

'Yeah, it.'

Tex turned her head from the words. I pondered on the state of my breath, then I pondered if drunks spat when they talked, then I pondered if the thought revolted her, then I just pondered 'IT.' As if emphasis cleared up the definition quicker.

Tex remained close, probably because she was still

within my grip. I could feel the warmth rising from her skin. Her fragrance drifted through my nostrils. She was sweet like strawberries. Mmm strawberries they'd be nice right now. Oh, dipped in chocolate that's even better. Yes chocolate.

Lost in thought about chocolate I hadn't realised that Tex had moved in closer. Her nose skimmed across mine. It made me want to laugh. Her lips brushed my cheek. They were soft and plump like strawberries. Mmm strawberries they'd be nice right now. Oh, dipped in ...

The sensation of her lips pressing against mine removed any thought about anything. And then all was dark.

~ 12 ~

'I haven't seen you in these parts before.' Enquired the hairdresser staring at his own hair in the mirror. He flicked the glittered tendrils before returning his gaze to Clare.

'No. I'm just passing through.'

'What's the plan for your hair today?'

Asks the hairdresser hopefully as he runs his fingers through Clare's long strands, flicking them out here and there. His eyes questioning in the mirror's reflection. Waiting for his talent to be wasted, the hairdresser starts to lose interest in Clare and refocuses on his own hair.

Clare bites her lower lip. 'I want a complete change. I don't want to be me anymore.'

The hairdresser looks a little shocked, and then displays his excitement through a small hand clap. 'Goodie. I love a challenge. Trust me darling I will make it so your own mother wouldn't recognise you.'

Excellent thought Clare. In a way it had been a hard decision to leave, in so many others it wasn't. Harry had made the final choice for her, regrettably Clare had always known it was a possibility. She had been saving a small stash of cash for years. Putting it away in a shoe box in her wardrobe for some rainy day.

Now that she had left there was nothing she wanted

from Harry, not even their shared investments. Harry would survive, she was a true survivor. Now Clare just had to ensure that she survived the best she could.

'So darling, before we begin, two things. Your name and what colour?'

The hairdresser let out an excited squeal.

'CJ. My name's CJ. And anything that's not dull.'

Obviously, the right answer as the hairdresser squealed again, clapped his hands and left for the colour bar.

Clare looked in the mirror and took a final glance at who she was. She was hoping in an hour she would be someone completely different. At least on the outside, for that would be a start. The inside would take more time and more work.

~ 13 ~

The morning sun snuck through the crack in the curtains. It startled my eyes making me want to dive deep within the covers. Stretching I felt a small ache in my back. I realised I was alone on the bed and sighed. My mind still hazy. Very little of last night was coming through. Something about strawberries, I think.

Peering out from the covers I realise for the first time that this room has only one bed, and I'm in it. Looking around I can see my bag and Tex's duffle, however no Tex. I listen out for the shower, no bathroom noises are heard. The birds outside are loud. Too loud. Their squawking rattles through my head.

Using my hands to raise my body I manage to swing my legs off the bed. I teeter there for a while before I can actually stand. In fact, it takes me three attempts before I'm finally on my feet. Grabbing my sunglasses from the side table I shuffle to the curtains. The darkened lenses do not seem sufficient against the fireball we call the sun. Make note to self: buy darker sunglasses.

After my pupils have scampered shut, I am just able to make out the feint outline of Tex in the car park. She is leaning on the side mirror of a pick-up truck. My eyes are a millimetre between being squinted and being shut. I strain them to make out the figure in the car. It's the bar girl from the distillery.

Tex smiles her lopsided smile, steps back from the vehicle, then waves to the girl. The pick-up drives away, leaving Tex standing alone in the car park, with her camera in hand. For some reason I feel a pinch in my gut. A niggle of some sort. When Tex turns to face the room, I quickly draw the curtains shut.

Refusing breakfast, my stomach just couldn't take it; Tex has us on the road to Rockhampton. She smiles as she drives. Whistling a tune every now and then. Smiling at me often, asking if I'm feeling okay. Knowing I didn't!

We make a quick pit stop in Gladstone for a bite, and a photo op at the 360-degree views at Round Hill lookout, before we continue on to Rockhampton. Tex's mood was high, and I must admit mine was lifting. When we hit Rocky, I had to drive as Gertie was a little confused. Can't blame her it is a funny spot we are heading to. My parents live in a speckle of a town on the Fitzroy River not far from Goodedulla National Park. Nearby are places called The Ridge and The Caves. Compared to the aboriginal names the white settlers weren't very creative.

This is familiar land for me. A mix of farming, national parks and forests. It brings back memories, good and bad. It's been dry, some may call it a drought, so the dust is thick. It settles on the back of your throat, in your hair and cakes in your nostrils. To me it smells of home. I look across to Tex who is no longer lounging. Her lanky form is tightly pressed to the windscreen hoping to catch her first glimpse of home. My childhood home.

'That must be it!'

Tex is excited. Her finger points to a gate that has an old milk can painted like a plump corgi. Old iron from a rusted water tank is cut into the shape of legs, a tail and ears.

'How'd you guess?' I murmur sarcastically though she ignores me. Instead she reaches for her phone and dials.

'Mum we're here!' Then promptly hangs up.

'Stop. Stop Gill. I need a shot of this.'

The milk can corgi is used to a few photos from lost travellers, however this is the first time it has been taken advantage of from so many angles. I swear I saw it smile. From there it was just a short drive along the dirt drive-way. Within moments the Queenslander house that had been my childhood home came into view. It sat on its little stumps allowing the breeze to pass underneath. More than once I had hidden within the dirt under the house building tracks for my toy horses to run freely on. The corrugated iron roof flowed from the highest peak onto the veranda which surrounded the whole house. I loved that tin roof. I remember when one of the worst droughts had broken, the rain sounded like dancing fairies. At first it sounded like them sneaking onto the roof then when it got heavier it sounded like they were doing an Irish jig.

Out of the bull nose veranda step my mother and my father. Charles the corgi remains in the cool embrace of the shade. Before I have managed to put the car in park, Tex is down the short front path surrounded by wildflowers embracing my mother. MY mother.

'Has she been looking after you?'

As I turn to answer I see that mother is talking to Tex. She's holding her at arm's length. I now missed that annoying little habit that used to be focused on me.

'She been feeding you okay, you look a little drawn.'

'I'm fine.' Murmurs Tex with a coy smile.

'Mr Delene.' Tex offers a hand, dad embraces her with a hearty chuckle.

'Call me dad.'

'Gillian.'

Yay, mum finally acknowledges my existence.

'Take the bags into your old room while we show Tex around.'

What? Where are my hugs and greetings? I stumble with the bags, cursing every moment. Even Charles the corgi snubs me as I cross the veranda. That or he is sleeping except I thought I heard a small growl, or snore, or maybe it was a snicker.

When I enter the house, a familiar fragrance assaults me. A mix of Mr Sheen wood polish and eucalypt floor wash. My nostrils flare in anticipation of reaching my room. As a child Mum always spread lavender in my drawers, and the smell became entrenched in everything. To me it offered a sense of warmth and security.

The best part about going home, especially when you are an only child, is that your parents leave your room as it was. In some ways, I find it refreshing to step into my childhood sanctuary. Sure, being a kid has its down points, although your room was and will always be whatever you want it to be. A castle where you fight dragons, I told you my father wanted a son! A tree house where you, and all the jungle animals, hide out. So what if the vicious animals are just stuffed with wadding?

As I swing open the door my heart skips a beat, my breathing becomes rapid and my hand quivers on the doorknob.

'Like what I've done?' Mother magically appears behind me. 'That room had been childish for so long. No point really, especially since there aren't any grandkids.'

My vision blurs slightly as I scan the room. My teenage posters are gone. Blink 182. Pink. Gwen Stefani. All replaced with a fresh coat of blue paint. The single princess bed has been replaced with a double. Stumpy the giraffe and all his friends are gone. I can feel the blood pulsating at my temples. Just breathe.

'Plus, we needed a proper guest room especially since you were bringing Tex. I can't imagine the two of you being romantic in a monkey wallpapered bedroom.'

The monkeys are gone? Romantic? With Tex? Mother! Is she speaking about sex before marriage? Wouldn't the soul be cast into the fires of hell? Where is my mother? What have you done with her? Mother lowered her voice as if she was sharing a secret with me.

'Plus, we assumed this one must be special as you've never brought anyone home, ever.'

'Looks great mum.' Is all I can manage as Tex squeezes past. Really? Never ever brought anyone home? I suppose I've never been good at even having a relationship let alone finding someone to introduce to them.

'I've got your parcel here somewhere.' States Tex as she

relieves me of the bags. Rustling through her duffle she finds it. 'Aha, here it is.'

'You are fantastic dear. How much do I owe you?'

'Nothing. You're family.' Responds Tex.

Here I was thinking that this was my family. Stupid me. 'Really? No, no, dear.'

Tex insisted, mother looked surprised but left smiling as she did so.

As mother vanished from view, Tex's attention diverted to me.

'This is an awesome place. Your parents are awesome.' She paused momentarily to take in the picture of me still standing in the doorway, hand on doorknob and mouth agape. 'You okay, Gill?'

'Sure.'

I respond though my childhood sanctuary is no more. My parents think she is a part of the family. My lie has grown into a weed that has swallowed me whole. Tex studies me with her eyes then raises the camera. She takes two shots. One straight away and one after her question.

'Why do you act like you're so hard done by Gill? You're neurotic about it? Your life wasn't difficult. You have parents that love you.'

How do you describe to someone who has had no real connection to their parents, or anyone else for that matter, what the feeling of failure is? The expectations placed in the unspoken words. The looks of disapproval. The tut tuts when they can't bear to voice their disappointment. The talks of dreams and success that you fail to bring to fruition. How do you voice the words of failure, especially to the people you love most? You respect most. You want to please most.

I was so lost in thought I failed to hear the clicking of the camera.

'Do you know how incredibly sad you looked just then?'

Tex moves closer and places her hand on my cheek. Her eyes are attempting to pierce mine, to find the thoughts behind them.

'Why Gill?'

A small single tear escapes from my right eye. Tex gently brushes it away with her thumb. I have a desperate desire to change the subject.

'What'd you get mum? In the paper bag?'

'You really have to ask her Gill.'

The moment was becoming uncomfortable, so I took leave of the situation and headed towards my mother's room. Like a small child I knock before entering. My parent's bedroom had always been their sanctuary. I was never allowed to barge in. As a child this was inconvenient, now I realise the respite such a sanctuary could offer. Especially now that mine had vanished.

'Oh Gillian. I'm so glad you liked the room. Your father and I were a little worried you'd be disappointed.'

'No mum its fine.'

Disappointed? How? I'm the child. I'm the disappointment. My mother turns to hug me. For a moment I thought she was going to say something, for her mouth opened slightly. She must have thought better of it as she returned to the brown paper bag on the bed.

'Quickly, shut the door.'

Taken by surprise I did as she said.

'I don't want your father seeing this, at least not yet.'

Her conspiratory grin said more than I could read. Oh, I thought, it's a present for dad. I wonder why Tex didn't just say that.

'What do you think?'

What do I think? I was aghast. My face must have looked aghast.

'Don't be such a prude Gillian.'

A prude! A prude! It's not every day that your mother pulls out a dildo. Quite a large one at that. And one that a lesbian has bought her.

'I'm so glad she got the colour I wanted.'

Yes, yes, the colour makes all the difference. Easily concealed amongst the pot plants I'm sure. Bright green! Great for an article in better homes and dildos.

'Do you know what it is?'

Stupid, stupid, question I suppose. Do I really want the answer?

'Of course, dear.'

Mother looks at me a little concerned.

'You are a strange one at times.'

With a chuckle she takes the offending device and tucks it into her sock drawer.

'I suppose the two of you are hungry? I better get something together.'

As we turn to leave the room, I pray my mother washes her hands before handling the food. Actually, I pray she washes them many times before touching the food. Actually, I think I've lost my appetite.

$$\sim 14 \sim$$

The metal was cold against her temple. The sun had risen and fallen, still Harry had not moved. For an unknownth time she lowered the pistol and studied it again. This time she let her tongue taste the coldness. It sent a shiver up her spine. It made her fillings ache. Her lips rested on the curve of the barrel.

Shutting her eyes Harry wondered at what force the bullet could enter her body. She jolted her head back in mock impact. Taking the gun from her mouth she looks at the wall behind her. Studying it she rises, gun still in hand, and removes the painting. Harry returns to her original position checking the spot where the painting had been.

Resting it in her lap, she studies the gun once again. Her finger strokes the grip feeling the criss-cross that was etched there. Ejecting the ammo clip, Harry examines an exposed bullet.

Her mind skips rapidly, excitedly at times. How far is it from existing to not existing? Harry surmises it's about half an inch. In a different frame of mind, that's the distance her finger would take to press for an elevator, to strike a match or to tickle a lover. That very same finger, at the start of her life's journey, pointed with breathless wonder at the stars and moon above. Half an inch is all it had to travel to end it all.

She recalls the statistics for female suicide with a gun. They were low compared to male counterparts. Harry wondered if this was a vanity thing or for the fact of the mess it would make. Was that why she removed the painting?

Gun laws had tightened in the last few years making it harder for everyday people to get hold of an unregistered piece. Her great uncle had adamantly refused to hand his prized possessions in when the government offered a financial incentive to anyone who handed in a gun, any shape, any form. He'd tucked away this pistol in a shoebox. Before his death he had tucked away many shoeboxes each with a relative's name on it. It wasn't only the law he didn't trust, it was lawyers too. Upon his death a relative innocently had handed Harry the box with her name on it. Her inheritance as such.

She checks the exposed spot where the painting had hung. She recalls her choices. She recalls her aggression. She recalls her love. Harry realises that recognising your soul mate at such a young age was not necessarily advantageous. Though the love stayed strong and the common memory bank grew, personal self-development was often stunted. She doesn't blame Clare, in fact, Harry blames herself. The drinking, the senseless angry sex with other women, all in a hope to cure the underlying anger in herself. These were choices she made.

Clare always encouraged Harry to reach for her dreams, although Harry never deemed herself able to leap at risks. She sought security. Therefore, she lay stunted, unable to grow, unable to develop into the person Clare had seen her to be, expected her to be.

Sobbing Harry rests her face in her hands. The left still held the gun. Its metal body was absorbing the warmth of her cheek. Clare had every right to leave but to commit suicide? That, in Harry's eyes, was the most selfish act. And pointless. Once again, she recalled statistics. Women find it easier to overdose.

The mobile phone, which sat across from her, rang, startling Harry from her thoughts. Automatically she answers it.

'Ms Granger this is Sergeant Beilby. I don't want to get your hopes up, there has been a possible sighting of Clare. We are currently following the leads.'

Harry was in two minds over this new information. Statistics ran through her head again. The gun was as warm as she. Fuck statistics she thought.

~ 15 ~

The presentation of Charles the corgi's championship ribbon was a proud moment for my dad. Tex captured his achievement on film, or digital, or whatever it is these days. I think even Charles carried himself a little taller as he passed the other corgis.

Mum gushed over both, even celebrating with a bottle of champagne. As a special treat she had sewn a new bed for Charles the corgi in the championship colours. In one corner his initials were also sewn into the fabric. Tex fussed over the stupid dog too. Every time I leant in for a pat Charles growled mischievously under his breath.

After the champagne my parents retreated to their room and made quite a ruckus. Quite disturbing for any child really. At one point my mind drifted to the bright green.... No. No! I wish I had never seen it or been privileged to its existence.

'Is there anything to do in Speckle at night?'

Tex sat on the end of the floral lounge looking at me. Her eyes pleaded with me to save her.

'There's a few clubs in Rocky or Yeppoon.'

I had snuck into one or two once when I was underage. Clare was with me. That makes me wonder what Clare is up to and whether she has returned. I make a mental note to call her.

'They're okay I suppose.'

'Well it's that or this.'

Her head tilted towards the ruckus coming from my parent's room.

We both practically sprinted from the house and leapt into the Jeep. Tex's laughter flowed behind us. I must admit I found the situation quite amusing too. Our mad dash brought us to a nightclub in the centre of Rockhampton. It must have been an exclusive club as there was a small line outside, held back by a thick velvet cord tethered to chrome bollards. Tex strode in like she owned the place, skipping the line without a thought. Wolf whistles followed Tex's curves. I trailed after her. The bouncer, gave me a head to toe check, was about to refuse entry until Tex stated I was with her.

I was with her. The way she said it, it was so forceful, so claiming, so unusual, for me at least. A little bust thrust here and there, and Tex and I had enough drinks for an hour. Someone yelled 'Yee haw Tex,' from across the room although I couldn't make out who it was. Tex waved and smiled her lopsided smile.

'Come Gill, time to dance.'

Tex leapt from the barstool and grabbed my hand. As I protested, she dragged me through the crowd to the centre of the floor. Tex danced freely however one could mistakenly call the action seductive movement to music. My eyes were fascinated with her fluid motion. The swivel of her hips, the arch of her back, the jiggle of her breasts. Hypnotised by the dance I was unsure whether Tex was moving to the music or whether it was moving to her. Others must have thought the same as a small circle formed around us.

My body tried to imitate hers, although my hips had the jerkiness of the tinman and my arms flailed as if scaring crows. I gave up when others swarmed in and I found myself on the edge of the dance floor. Shrugging I went to the bar.

'What'll it be hotcakes?'

The bartender spoke loudly over the music. I waited till he finished serving whoever he was speaking to.

'What'll it be?'

Suddenly I realise he is talking to me. His smile is warm and welcoming. I stutter nervously while asking for a cranberry and vodka.

'Slice of lemon?'

All I could do was nod.

'You don't come around here much. New in town?'

'No. Visiting home. My parents live in Speckle.'

He laughed as did I, then I corrected myself and told him of the town my parents live in.

'Speckle. Lots of those towns around here. Good name.'

A blonde lent across the bar revealing her well-endowed proportions. Licking her lips, she asked for a drink.

'Service please.' Yelled the bartender to another who immediately ran to serve the woman. She looked a little disappointed.

'You came with the cowgirl?'

Finally, we were getting to the point of his attention. He was after Tex's details. I felt like throwing my drink in his face, though I didn't. I thought about it long and hard.

I chose to snub him instead. As I turned my back he spoke again.

'Whoa hotcakes. You aren't getting away that easy.' He leapt the bar as the words left his mouth.

'My name's Pete.'

'Gillian.' I mumbled.

'Want to grab a drink with me outside?'

Though this was the best proposal I'd had in a long time, and he was rather cute, handsome really, I paused for a moment. Pete waved to a girl in the distance. At the same moment one moved behind him, sliding her body against his. Apologising as she went. Pete grabbed my arm and began to lead me outside. As we reached the door, I was surprised to see Tex.

'She's with me.' Her voice was flat and firm.

'We were just going to have a drink outside.' Pete protested. I stood dumbfounded.

'I don't think so.'

As she spoke Tex knocked the drink from my hand just as I was about to take a sip. She glared at Pete as she took my arm and led me away.

'Gill.'

She scolded although I had no idea what she scolded me for. She pushed me into the passenger side of the Jeep and shut the door. As she seated herself in the driver's side, she gave me a pitiful look.

'Don't you know bartenders are the worst?'

Worst at what I thought. I'm sure Tex talks in riddles. I recall that conversation we had the first morning at my house. This was similar.

'Fresh meat.' She continued. Fresh meat? Hmm that was new. What sort of fresh meat I wondered?

'Did you watch his hands as he made the drink?'

'No. Why?'

Her sigh was another scolding. I really sucked at this didn't I?

'Gill, it was spiked?'

'No. There was no pineapple in it. No spikiness.'

'Drug spiked Gill.'

'Really?'

Wow, never had that before. Does this mean he liked me or not? I was about to ask but thought better of it. Tex didn't seem too pleased with the whole thing.

Gertie, the GPS, was sprouting left and rights in the background. I thought she was leading us home. She wasn't. Tex pulled up on a ridge overlooking the lights of Rockhampton. At night it was quite spectacular. Tex found a blanket in the back and several bottles of fruit wine that we had picked up in Bundaberg and forgotten about. Stretching out her lanky body, Tex invited me to join her.

'You're not very experienced in the world, are you?'

'Gee thanks.'

I plopped down next to her ensuring there was enough space between us. I wondered what was worse: Pete with his spiked drink or Tex with her barbed tongue.

'It's not such a bad thing Gill. Quite refreshing, you should embrace it.'

Embrace naivety? Who had ever heard of that? I studied her briefly as she adjusted her hat back. Catching my gaze, she smiled and placed her hat on my head.

'How 'bout you be me for a while?'

A soft sad laugh followed the words. The hat sat snugly on my head. I adjusted it this way and that, making Tex laugh all the while.

'Great, then you can be me!'

Why would anyone want to be me I wondered? Maybe Tex was right when she called me neurotic. It had stung at the time though I thought it over. Yes, the thought rolled and rolled in my head for ages. Most thoughts do.

Tex was halfway through a bottle of wine by the time I abandon my thoughts. She offers me the remainder, her eyes daring me to scull it. I do and quickly regret it. Tex feigns shock which makes me laugh which also makes wine shoot out of my nostrils. This leaves both of us in hysterical laughter. I let my body crash backwards on the rug. Taking in the stars I ponder about the universe. Tex ponders about the next bottle of wine.

I hear a pop then I see her above me tipping the bottle. Mouth open wide I attempt to catch the falling nectar. Due to her unsteady hand, or my unsteady head, some spills down my neck. More splatters on my forehead and even more drizzles onto my chest. Taking a gulp from the bottle Tex yells 'don't waste it' and dives in.

Her tongue laps the wine fragments from my head then follows the trail down my neck. As she passes my ear, I'm sure she takes a nibble. Oh no, no, no, not the ear. Electric shivers combined with the wine, makes me giggle nervously. Taking a deeper breath Tex dives towards my lower neck brushing the top of my chest. At the hollow, at the bottom of my throat she makes slurpy sounds. This makes me laugh even louder.

Her mouth is warm. While her teeth nibble, her eyelashes tickle my skin. Nibbling up my neck her nose puffs warm air into my ear. Tex is above me and on me in the same motion. One of her hands strokes my arm, while the other brushes through my hair to support my head.

Subconsciously my hands wander. Each moving up an exposed arm. It feels out of body as if I was watching from above, like a movie. Gillian has stepped out leaving ... Gill? As my left hand rounds the knob of her shoulder it hesitates before tracing the line of Tex's vest, right into the cleavage. Tex's breath hastens in my ear. My own breath hastens.

Freezing momentarily my body is unsure of what to do. A gasp escapes my mouth then is replaced with Tex's lips. Firstly, she nips my top lip, then my bottom. Seductively her mouth encompasses mine. I feel like screaming. For joy or for shock I am unsure. Tickling the tip of my tongue, her tongue distracts me from any further thought.

The weight of her is on me now. Gently pushing down from above. Hesitating momentarily then continuing. Her body against mine is soft. It smelt sweet, like strawberries. Mmm strawberries they'd be nice right now. Oh, dipped in chocolate that's even better. Yes chocolate. Hang on. Have I been here before?

Deepening with each movement the kiss was all consuming. Eradicating thought and self in one motion. I felt good. Was that bad?

It must have been bad because Tex lifts slightly, takes in my mouth and eyes, then removes herself from me. It is a quiet trip home.

The decision wasn't that hard thought Clare, who now preferred to be called CJ. Especially since she had no home. The Volkswagen Kombi Camper was oldish, yet it appeared to be in good working condition.

'See, it has a gas stove and fridge. Both in working condition.'

The salesman spoke with a lack of interest. He was keen to get rid of this heap, however he wasn't sure about this woman who had walked out of nowhere. Next, he demonstrated the pop top and the fold out bed. As they both stood in the van, he did show some embarrassment when the bed was pulled out. Coughing, the salesman quickly demonstrated how it returned into place making a back seat.

'Looks okay. Interesting colour.' Stated Clare observing the mix of grey primer and baby poo yellow.

All the salesman could do is shrug.

'$5000 take it or leave it.'

To leave it would mean Clare would have to continue walking. To take it meant she would have a new home to go with the new her.

'I'll give you four thousand in cash right now.'

Bolstered by her new look, Clare feigned confidence to bully the salesman who she knew would be keen to bully her. With a slight laugh the salesman nods his head and offers his hand to seal the deal.

~ 17 ~

Her eyes were heavy, intoxicated from the night be-fore. Blinking, the fogginess failed to vanish. Even with immense effort Harry was unsure whether she could get her head to move from the pillow. After five attempts she raised it enough to swing her legs over the bed.

Peering to the side Harry could see a naked woman sound asleep next to her. This wasn't the woman she had succumbed to in the bar's bathroom. They must have met later in the night after even more drinks. Harry shrugged; she really didn't care either way.

She wondered when she had brought her home. Though upon closer inspection of the surroundings she realised she wasn't even at home. The room was stark in colour and decoration, a sure sign that she was in a hotel.

On the floor lay her clothes ripped from her body in a moment of passion she guessed. As her legs weren't ready to be weight bearing, Harry used her toes to collect each article of clothing. With effort she managed to dress seated. Finally, she had to stand to fix her jeans.

Repelled by her own breath Harry took a swig of some liquid out of a glass on the night stand. Swirling it in her mouth she tasted its bitterness before spitting it back into the glass. Stale alcohol. Then again mouth wash is based on alcohol she reasoned.

Stumbling to the door, Harry turned to view the woman again. She was vaguely familiar. Sam was the name that came to mind though Harry was sure no introduction was made last night. Hanging from the dresser Harry made out a uniform; emergency services. Yes, Sam was her name. Harry recalled her now. She was a cheat, well known amongst Harry's other friends. Left her wife at home in Sydney while she went on business trips to Brisbane. Sam had been doing this for ten years, assuming no one knew. Harry guessed that most of the trips ended like this. A non-descript woman in a non-descript room.

Harry too had cheated. So, she was a cheater with a cheater. How sad. The poor women they leave behind. Harry thought about Clare. How innocent. How beautiful. She had trusted Harry when she was supposed to be working late. Had trusted her unconditionally. And what had Clare gained from that? Possibly a premature death, all alone. Harry despised herself even more.

Taking a last look at the woman, bile rose up in Harry's mouth. It was acidic, burning her tongue and cheeks. Last she heard this woman's wife had just had a child. Harry barely shut the door behind herself as vomit flew from her mouth, landing on the closest indoor plant.

~ 18 ~

It took me by surprise, I happily accepted my mother's offer of an outing to the hairdresser. Tex wasn't invited and this excited me even more. The night before had been strange. The nightclub. The lookout. Dare I say it, the kiss. Currently I was more intrigued with the moment at hand.

There's not too much to do in Speckle much like many outback towns. It has a pub, a grocery store, a town hall, a hairdresser, another pub and a post office. Not much else really. Those tourists who do make it to Speckle are always lost on their way to somewhere else.

The town still had that traditional feel. It always amused me when I saw tourists taking photos next to the horse hitching posts outside many of the businesses. They assumed they existed from fifty plus years ago except the people in Speckle still used them. Many a retired farmer rode their prized quarter horse into town on a Sunday for coffee or a pint of beer.

The greeting at the hairdressers was cheery and warm. The windows were clean and fresh so as to provide the occupants a good view of the street and both corner pubs. Inside was like a time capsule. Posters of new hairstyles from various decades slathered the wall behind the wash stations like posters on a teenager's room. None were ever removed though more were continually added until it was a collage of hairdressing history. The hair wash stations were the original musky pink with matching chairs. Next to that were some full over the head hairdryers. The kind women sit oblivious under for hours, cross-legged, reading magazines and sipping coffee. Then there was a line of large leather salon chairs. Big and brass like with bulging backs. The line of sparkling mirrors seemed the only thing ever updated.

Amazingly entering the salon was not unlike when I was a child except that instead of being ushered to the small carpeted area, I was allowed in one of the big salon chairs. Due to the lack of a coffee shop most of the town's women congregated here. All of mum's cronies. The sitting area was full of them, all sipping filtered coffee, and when that area overflowed a couple filled the salon chairs.

Today I was in one of those chairs. There were six in total although only two were ever used for their purpose. Besides there was only one hairdresser and on occasion one trainee. Generally, the trainee was a local girl saving up for something. Most likely a way out of Speckle.

'Oh, Jilly it's been so long. Do you remember me? I used to cut your hair when you were small.'

'Yes, Miss Trombone, I remember you.'

Hopefully that was my sweetest smile. There is no way I could offend one of mum's cronies.

'Call me Betty dear. Now that you are a big girl.'

Yes, a big girl still under the shadow of my mother. I think? This trip has been peculiar.

'What would you like done dear?'

'Well.'

My mother started before I could say anything. I could only imagine what she was going to say. I quickly interject.

'Just cut the split ends and tidy it up please.'

'Really?'

Mother looked at me a little strange.

'I thought you'd go a little, well, shorter.'

'Shorter?'

Shorter. Why would I go shorter? It took me forever to grow to this length. The city hairdresser, sorry stylist, said it framed my face well.

'Oh, that would be perfect.'

Betty was excited. This scared me. What would a retiree know about city hair let alone short city hair?

'Yes shorter.'

Mum's voice was firm and sure.

'Mum!'

I squealed. In a not so hushed tone, she justified her request.

'Aren't you the boy in the relationship?'

The boy! The boy! What did she mean by that? I've never been so insulted in my life. Now my mother didn't think I could hold down the female role in a relationship. What had my life become? If JoJo was here, I wonder what he'd say. Or what he'd make a swan out of.

The ladies in the crowd agreed. Short. A vote was taken and apparently, I wasn't allowed an opinion. So, everyone knows about my life?

'Have you told her?' Whispered another.

'Not yet.' Hushed another.

Told me what? That they've all decided I need a sex change or something. My father always wanted a son. The thought of being a man slightly appealed. Being a new person. Maybe I could start again. I wonder if I'd be a better son than daughter? The pressure of grandchildren would no longer lie on me. That would go to my wife. My wife? What am I talking about? Oh, my goodness, does my mother expect me to marry Tex?

'Well.'

Betty prompted.

'Gillian. We were thinking.'

With those words she waved her hand around the salon.

'All the other little local towns have some festival. You know like the watermelon festival. Thong throwing. Stump carving.'

'Aha.'

I nodded although it really didn't make sense.

'Well we were thinking we could put our own little town on the map with a festival.'

'Sounds awesome mum.'

What were they thinking? A little knitting festival. A gossip carnival.

'We're glad you're excited about it. We've decided to have one of those parades. You know with the floats.'

The excitement was gurgling amongst all of them.

'We've been thinking of this for a while, yet we only just decided on a theme recently. We even started advertising a few weeks ago.'

A theme sounded good although what does that have to do with me? The disappointing daughter.

'Yes.'

Mother continued. The crescendo of chatter rose in excitement.

'We are going to have a gay pride festival.'

And then there was silence. All eyes watching me for a response.

My mouth went dry. I could barely swallow.

'Gay pride?'

'Yes dear. Ever since you told me your news. I discussed it with the girls, and we decided to commemorate you. Show our support and all that for your lifestyle choice. We want you to ride on the main float.'

This is the point when I obviously was meant to inject excitement. Instead I interjected a vacant block out for the next twenty minutes. By the time I came out of it I had a nice new haircut and a mother who was hugging me saying how proud she would be with me on the float. Just breathe.

Tex took the news as could be expected. Plentiful laughter followed by shock when mother asked her to lead the parade. She nearly choked on her peach cobbler. It amused me, I kept it to myself.

~ 19 ~

After purchasing the van Clare drove for a few hours away from anything that resembled home. All she knew was that she was fully into northern New South Wales now. One town took her fancy especially when she saw a 'ladies' night' sign hanging outside a building with a rainbow flag. She hoped the flag meant gay pride because she had no desire to walk in on a four year old's unicorn birthday party. The van was an easy set-up at the local showgrounds which was within walking distance of the bar. For good measure she popped into a local country outfitter, in fact the only clothes store in town, to get a new look to go along with her new hair. For even better measure she grabbed a chilled six-pack of vodka pre-mixers at the local bottle-o to help build courage for her planned night out.

Clare waltzed into the gay bar. Her boots clipped loudly on the wooden floor although they barely drew any attention. A few barflies, sitting at the alcohol-polished bar, passed a quick look her way. They didn't even register in Clare's vision as she had other things on her mind. Focused on her task, she headed straight for the jukebox. A small coin lay poised in her clenched palm; it hung momentarily over the slot as Clare stood in indecision between Melissa Etheridge and the Indigo Girls. Which would represent the new her? The raunchy, risk taking new Clare.

Upon deciding on which song would scream freedom, Melissa Ferrick's Drive, Clare let the coin clink into the slot. Raising her head, and without removing her sunglasses, she scanned the bar. Movement caught her attention at one of the back booths. A tall muscular woman stood over an engaging blonde in an intimidating way. As the woman's body bent lower to come face to face with the blonde Clare's view of the booth's occupant became blocked. Somehow Clare could sense the blonde's discomfort.

Such intimidation jerked at Clare's conscience. She herself had been a victim to such things. Harry's image jumped into her mind and as it grew so did her anger.

'Vic's at it again.' A nearby table stated

'Vic.' Muttered Clare to herself as she viewed this woman dressed in a stark white singlet, studded belt, jeans and steel cap work boots. Very stereotypical she thought. Her aggressiveness and tone reminded Clare of Harry's mannerisms. As Clare approached, she could hear Vic's words.

'Come on hun, it wouldn't hurt to dance while you're waiting.'

Vic gyrated her hips, before slicking down the sides of her hair and forcefully taking the girl's hand. The girl tried unsuccessfully to pull her hand back.

'I'm worth the risk.'

Clare stood poised for a moment before she spoke. Her

assessment of the situation appeared correct. It was a rapid clear voice that descended on the woman's ears.

'You messing with what's mine?' Allowing a pause to emphasis the words before she spoke again, Clare glared at Vic as she turned to view her tormentor. 'Cause I'd advise you not to.'

Inside she was shaking yet Clare wanted to be this person who appeared unbreakable.

Vic laughed, leaning forward she hooked her thumbs behind her belt buckle.

'And what of it, bitch.'

Twitching at the ends, Clare's pursed lips turned into a perverted sort of smile.

'Hmm.' Her head nodded for a few seconds and the words came again, this time in a whisper. 'Because you don't want to see me angry.'

'Hah!'

Vic scoffed loudly, while scanning the bar for an audience. Many eyes travelled her way thus giving her the confidence and desire to continue.

'Come on hun, I want to see you angry. Don't we all?'

She asked the bar in general. A few smirks echoed off the walls, Clare's eyes failed to stray from Vic. So Vic continued hoping to fill the silence.

'All for this piece of meat?'

'That bit of meat, as you shamelessly refer to her, is mine. And I've come to collect what's mine.'

Cold hard-bitten eyes focused on Vic. Sending an obvious chill down her spine as very few dared to stand against her. The room quietened in expectation.

Vic, indignant, rose to her full height before speaking again.

'I prefer something a little bit tastier.' Her smirk revealed her pleasure at her supposed smart wittedness.

'So, your hand is tastier than this gorgeous creature sitting behind you?'

Remaining passive, Clare's face took in the other woman. A few muffled laughs circled the room. Agitated, Vic's eyes failed to settle in one location for long. They flashed from Clare to the audience she herself had aroused. Her words came quickly, running into each other, creating a stuttering affect.

'That is not what I said. I said.'

'It's okay we all heard you and understood. You prefer your own hand.'

Her tone condescending, Clare continued, she was starting to enjoy this role.

'I would love to enter into an intellectual debate with you, but then again it is so dissatisfying to do it with someone who is so obviously ill equipped.'

Moving before Vic could get another word in, Clare reached her hand across the booth's table.

'Now if you don't mind, I have something to say to my woman.'

A woman who Clare had never met. She laughed nervously to herself. Grabbing the blonde, Nikki, by the wrist, Clare forced her to rise. Turning, she gave a quick rocking horse smile to the bewildered Vic, before leading Nikki away. As they made their way past the jukebox, the song

Clare had selected began to play. With a heavy sigh, Clare turned to Nikki.

'Why waste a perfectly good coin. Dance?'

Nikki's smirk was all the response needed. Pressing her close, Clare held Nikki tightly. Their cheeks brushed lightly as their breath mingled between them. Dipping her head slightly, Nikki's eyes came to rest on Clare's forehead. Smiling to herself, Clare gripped Nikki tighter. This was a new sensation for her. Life was totally full of Harry, now it wasn't. A momentary sadness filled her, fortunately it passed quickly. Their bodies swayed in unison, pressed together as if they were one. The warmth of another was something she missed.

Reluctantly the embrace was released when the song ended. Linking Nikki's hand in her hand, Clare led her outside. The brightness of the streetlights contrasted greatly with the darkness of the bar. Their eyes flickered, adjusting to the change of light. Searching up and down the avenue, Clare puckered her lips in indecision.

'Where are we going?' Nikki asked laughingly.

'Shhh.'

Clare's mind screamed in her head. She had never, never done this before. Both stood quiet, transfixed by the evening sky. Clare's voice finally broke the silence.

'To my van.'

With a tug, Nikki was soon trotting behind her without question.

The process of creating a festival was already in full swing before Tex and I had been informed of anything. Invitations to gay friendly groups had been posted. Advertisements had been prominent in many GLBT (Gay, Lesbian, Bisexual and Transgender) newspapers and journals. Apparently from my first conversation with my mother, in regard to my 'sexuality', I had set the ball in motion for this grand parade.

Me! It was all my fault just because I lied about being gay. The ripple effect I've been told. My mother had handled the news as best as she could. Needing a shoulder to lean on she had spoken about it to one friend who had spoken about it to another. And so forth and so on. Finally, when mother made an appearance at the salon, all the cronies had a story about a gay relative or friend. Mum was not alone. Solidarity was the inspiration for the theme of the festival. Gay pride. Or as mum put it 'comfortable in your own skin.'

Personally, I think it is a great theme. Especially for so many closeted country folks like my parents. Come to think of it, maybe country folk are more open. I've been in the city so long, maybe I am the one with blinkers on. It will bring life and colour to such a dull Speckle. An influx of much needed cash too. The town was expected to swell from 271 locals to over two thousand people. The only true issue is me riding pride of place on the main float. Me. The not so gay lesbian.

Mother made many interesting suggestions. The worst being Tex and I in wedding clothes. I think Tex took a moment to consider that one! How strange. Tex after the initial shock actively started encouraging my mother. I was aghast.

'You know it's actually nice that your mother wants to do this for you.'

Tex lay in our bed watching me trying to plump up my short hair.

'To me you mean.'

My hair was so short. I don't think I was even born with such short hair. Looking to the right and left I wondered if there was anything, I could do to improve it.

'Gill, stop playing with it and come to bed. Your new doo makes you look kinda sexy.'

Tex was patting the bed. Her hat swung limply from the side lamp.

'Great. Kinda sexy. To men or women Tex?'

I was trying to be sarcastic for my mother thought I was the boy in the relationship. The boy! Did this mean that my luck with men was going to get worse? Men. I was starting to think I didn't need one.

'To me.'

Tex's lopsided smile was solely focused on me. A slight twinkle flashed through her eyes.

Tex thinks I'm sexy? Me? Sexy? That doesn't compute. She is the sexy one with those curves. And last night's kiss that was so unbelievable. The most incredible kiss I've ever had, I felt it all through my body. What?

'Thanks.'

Breathe deep. What am I thinking? Change of subject. Breathe!

'I'm just going to try Clare; I haven't spoken to her in ages.'

It felt like forever. There was so much I had to tell her. Surely, she would understand my dilemma. There wasn't a time I could recall that I didn't have her to confide in. Clare was my pillar in a sea of ... hmm ... what would one put here? Sea of non-excitement. Sea of instability. Sea. Makes me think of barnacles and algae. So, if she is my pillar am I a pesky barnacle?

I waited for ten rings, Clare did not answer. No voice mail either. That was strange, so I dialled Harry. No answer there either. Harry had seemed a little down while Clare was away. I bet she whisked Clare on a tropical holiday on her return. Harry was romantic like that. They probably went somewhere remote to be alone.

'Is your sounding board not answering? Can't blame her, you have a lot of neurosis to translate.'

What? What! I have a lot of neurosis. Where does Tex get off on saying that? I have anxiety, plain and simple. I just don't like stressful situations. In reality, my whole life is a stressful situation, well currently anyway.

'What is wrong with communicating with a friend?' I justify.

'And blubbering all of your so-called woes?' Tex responds.

The eyes of my pretend partner challenged me. Daring me to bite, to respond, to anything. And bite I did.

'Well if you were a loving caring partner then I would confide in you. Though your insensitivity abounds, it's not quite what I'm looking for.'

There! At least she had the sensibility to look slightly hurt. Tex's brow crinkled into a contemplative look. Her mouth opened, she paused. I gave her my best 'Well?' look.

'Well not all of us were lucky enough to have caring parents let alone parents who were around enough to even notice you.'

Blurts Tex though she recomposes herself quickly. It was true we knew very little about Tex's upbringing and had never heard any stories about her life before she met us.

Quiet filled the room and for the first time I could see pain in Tex's eyes. All I could do was move to where she sat and embrace her in my arms. Surprisingly she hugged me back.

'Sit.'

Tex murmured. I obliged. Sitting next to her she picked up my hand and placed it in the warmth of hers.

'Okay Gillian, let's discuss your dilemma?'

I nodded in response.

'Previously you were concerned that your mother wanted grandchildren from you, and soon.'

Nodding. D'uh, everyone knew that.

'You set up an elaborate plan to deter your mother from such a conclusion. That plan is currently in motion. Correct?'

'Yes.'

I murmured though I sensed she did not require a response.

'Now you are upset that your mother, who comes from a cloistered upbringing, has decided to support her daughter in her life choices. Not only that, she has convinced a town in the middle of nowhere, that they should demonstrate acceptance. And that town, Speckle, has decided to celebrate via a festival that will boost the town and the townspeople in so many ways.'

It sounds so different when Tex says it. She's absolutely right.

'All your mother is asking is that you ride on a float, for her. You have to do nothing. Your mother has not only rallied the town, she has organised this event from the ground up. Impressive for a country hick don't you think? You are the educated one. The one with all of the opportunities, with all of the support, yet you wallow in how hard you are done by. Tell me Gill, what is it that you really want?'

'I just want to be happy Tex.'

'We all do.'

'I want to be truly loved.'

'You are.'

Her arm swept around me as she drew me to her chest.

'Life often feels unfair, but you have to look at the positive. Find the funniness. Appreciate everything that is in front of you.'

Her body was warm against my cheek. Initially her heart pounded at a steady rhythm, now it was more rapid.

I took in her scent, it was sweet, like strawberries. Mmm strawberries, I love strawberries.

My hand was still clenched in hers. My cheek was pressed against her cleavage. Tex kissed the top of my head.

'Do you know how sweet you are Gill?'

Me sweet? Like strawberries? I don't think so. Tex's laugh bubbled over me.

'If you questioned the world as much as you questioned yourself you would be absolutely amazing.'

Me amazing? I doubt it. The point about questioning my self was true. Now that I think of it, I continually doubted myself too. Tex had found the one truth about me.

That single statement had me contemplating my life, the way I saw the world, the way I saw the people around me. Raising my head, I took a long look at Tex. Confusion showed on her face. In that moment, I saw the insecurities that grew in others. A weakness like my own however though the owner managed to minimise it slightly. Not fully through control. Not fully through suppression. Somewhere in between people found a strength to live with the weakness. Embrace it even.

This new knowledge brought a flurry of questions. I flopped on the bed next to Tex.

'So lover, tell me about your childhood?'

How else would I start such an intimate conversation? Tex's shocked faced revealed how taken back she was by the use of her favourite word. That or she was scared to talk about her childhood.

'What do you want to know?'

'Parents. Did you have any? Well I know you must have...'

'Yes, Gilly I had parents.'

Her face saddened and I felt pain for her although I did not know why. Her lips had downturned slightly and her eyes lost some sparkle.

'My mother. She was amazing. We used to go into the paddocks and pick wildflowers.'

'Sounds amazing.'

'Yes, she was. She loved animals. We had cats, dogs, goats, cows and horses, all strays; she'd find them, feed them up and find them homes or keep them. All the animals adored her. Followed her everywhere.'

Looking into the distance Tex paused.

'One day when I was five, we went for a walk near the river which ran along the back of our property. During the wet season the river would swell and come onto our property by a few metres. In the dry it would dip down. You know, same as it would around here.'

So, fascinated by the story all I could do was nod.

'This day the dry season just seemed to have started. We would go to the river to make sure no little fish were caught in the puddles. If they were, we'd scoop them up and put them back in the main water.'

A small laugh from the memory rolled from her lips.

'This day it was very muddy. My little legs sunk up to the knees in the mud. Mum had just rescued a few guppies and was a little further in. She was going to release them when she became stuck in the process. Stuck in the black slimy mud, how terrible. I tried to reach out to grab her hand so I could pull her out however I couldn't. I was too small.'

To be honest I was dreading where this story was going.

'Do you know how she got out?'

'No.' I said tentatively as she continued.

'One of the dumb cows she had rescued came down. He was a young Droughtmaster steer, with quite large horns. She just called his name and he took a few steps towards her, not even worrying about the mud even though his legs sunk like ours. That dumb cow put his head down and let her grab his horns and then he just yanked her right out of there!'

Tex seemed happy with the memory and the image seemed funny to me too.

'Anyway, my mother died a week later. A tumour on the brain they said.'

'I'm sorry.'

'It's okay it was a long time ago. She was amazing and I wonder how my life would have gone if she had lived.'

There was that distant stare again. I reached out and rubbed her arm in what I hoped was a soothing manner.

'And your dad?'

'My dad was a useless piece of crap. Never home. Never cared. He didn't understand my mother's love of those animals or how they loved her. He said they were a waste of feed. In fact, he served that poor dumb cow as a BBQ after the funeral. Mum would have hated it. I didn't eat meat for eight years after that.'

Tex is amazing really. She always held my gaze and as far as I know always told the truth. It was refreshing to receive unbridled honesty. It made me see her and myself in a new light. To lift the mood

'Okay, okay. What was your worst date?'

My curiosity was really piqued with this question. I was touching on a personal terrain I had never broached with anyone before. Without a pause Tex spoke.

'When Ginger bit me on the arse.'

'Bit you on the arse? Is that a thing?'

No laughter. No smile. I studied her eyes to see if she was for real.

'Really? What the hell were you doing?'

Oh no, do I really want to know? I was in such a flurry with questions that this was one I probably shouldn't have asked.

'Well, to be bitten on the arse I was obviously naked. I was appreciating a new friend when Ginger struck.'

'There were three of you?'

A bemused look was my response, then Tex spoke again.

'Ginger was a very large tabby cat. A very protective cat apparently.'

'A cat! Bit you on the arse? While you were doing it? OMG.'

'That wasn't the worst part of the date.'

'Really? There's worse? Is that possible?'

'The cat bite took me so by surprise, I flung forward hitting the bedhead, reeling me unconscious and I ended up in hospital.'

'OMG! I've led such a sheltered life.'

Laughter filled our lungs. It swarmed the room making us feel encased within it. It felt warm, refreshing and liberating.

~ 21 ~

Clare knew the night had been cold, frost crackled on the windows. Fortunately, it was on the outside not the inside of the Kombi. The warm breath within the van had fogged the back window. Reaching up Clare drew a heart. She added stitches and laughed.

The body beside her lay still under the half-drawn quilt. They had remained warm, what with the camper's insulation, as well as the vigorous activity that took place last night. Clare smiled. It was refreshing being someone else. Unusual yet refreshing. Tracing her finger along the chilled window, Clare could feel the fingertip going numb. When it was appropriately so, she traced the same finger down Nikki's back. The stranger was warm, like she remembered her.

Nikki stirred. Her tousled blonde hair made it hard to distinguish where her face was. Clare didn't mind, she leant in and kissed the mess.

'Good morning sunshine.' Spoke Nikki as her naked body stretched away the night's tension.

'Good morning.'

'Did I get your name yesterday?'

Nikki rose to one arm. The other swept the blonde mess aside. Her eyes were bluer than Clare remembered. Clare paused with indecision. In some places she had been

travelling on the name CJ, her initials, however this required adjusting to as she failed to respond to the name on
several occasions. The name was growing on her and she
felt it more edgy and adventurous than Clare ever was.

'CJ.'

She decided to keep it.

'Well CJ.'

Shaking her hand Nikki paused to kiss Clare's palm.

'I'm Nikki and I'd like to thank you for saving me from
a fate worse than death.'

'Worse than death? Really?'

'Well yes. I was rather drunk and there may have been
a possibility that Vic may have hauled me home with her.
Waking up next to her would have meant gnawing my arm
off. You know, coyote ugly and all.'

Clare laughed; she had never been in that situation.
In fact, she had never woken up with anyone other than
Harry. It wasn't horrible enough to gnaw your arm off,
quite the opposite. Harry seemed an experienced lover
even when she denied ever having any previous partners,
Clare always sensed she had. Clare felt her thoughts lingered too long on the topic of Harry so she returned them
to the woman at hand.

'Hungry?'

The question was innocent, Nikki took it into the lewd
by kissing down Clare's chest. She murmured yes as she
circled the belly button.

~ 22 ~

Mother and her Country Women's Group had been working exceedingly hard leading up to the festival. To assist, Tex had declared a girl's night in for the three of us. The thought of scrunching up on the floral couch with my mother and Tex was slightly disturbing especially since mother left the movie choice to Tex.

Unable to find anything suitable in Speckle, Tex had driven to Rockhampton. Her choice was unknown to mother and me although now I could hear it whirring in the DVD drive, waiting for our perusal.

'Your mother has seen the first one, so I had to find the second.' Tex was nonchalant.

'I love a good comedy.' Contributed mother.

Squeezed between the pair I sighed at the thought of something containing Renee Zell-whatever her name was. Or even worse Barbara Streisand. Tex offered me some popcorn. Mother was rubbing her hands together in excitement.

To say I was shocked was an understatement. When the Harold and Kumar title crossed the screen, I broke into a slight sweat. I remember seeing the first one in my house...alone. I had drawn the curtains, dimmed the lights, however I still felt as if I was doing something wrong. I had even taken the phone off the hook in case someone rang and I answered it without pausing the movie. The thought that one of my friends knew I was watching such porn. I would have died, yet here I was with my mother. My mother!! Isn't there some law against this?

The scene of naked women rising from the pool was near unbearable. In an attempt to avert my eyes, I had knocked the popcorn from Tex's lap. Splashed soda onto my mother and accidentally kicked Charles who had been sleeping at our feet.

'Gillian.' Mother had her stern voice on. 'They are just naked women.'

'She's just selective.' Laughed Tex as she paused the movie on a fully naked woman while I was trying to mop up the mess. It didn't help nor did her mischievous smile.

'Oh, it must be hard maintaining a bare lawn.' Stated mum seriously.

'Wax is popular.' Returned Tex.

Did neither of them see me here?

'Hmmm, I think just a trim is enough.' Mother countered.

What?! I can't handle this. I attempted to rise. Charles growled and nipped me on the heels.

'Yeah.' Chorused Tex. 'You don't want to be a wild woman.'

'Of Borneo.' Finished mother in unison.

That is it, my life is officially over. The mere thought of my mother's lawn. Aaagh! New thought. New thought. Happy thought.

I excused myself stating that the activity of the day had worn me out. I don't think either was listening, as their laughter blurred out my words. As I lay on my bed, feeling the cool of the evening I could hear the rumble of their laughter continue.

I went to the bathroom with the innocent thought of brushing my teeth and going to bed early. The toothpaste had run out so I rummaged in the cupboard looking for more. Laughing I pulled a variety of objects from the cupboard. My parents may have changed my room destroying my childhood sanctuary, however this little time capsule held an assortment of memories within grasp.

A plate which was promised to straighten out my bottom tooth on the left side. A quick look in the mirror reflected the failure. Next to that was a half empty tin of Impulse deodorant. The smell was sweet and salty like vomit at the sea was all that came to mind. Up the back was a small box with little hearts drawn on in gold pen. Gold pen, how amazing they were when they first came out. All shiny and metallic. The box creaked open to reveal a long-forgotten ring given to me by Tom in the eighth grade. How sweet that was. Hang on was that the last time I had a boyfriend? Happily, I can say no, not quite.

On the lower shelf was a little post pack tube. I had drawn Top Secret on the outside. After popping the lid, I found a rolled-up poster of ... gasp ... Heath Ledger! Him in his sunglasses – Mmm. With it was a love letter written in a hand writing that looked suspiciously like mine as a ten-year-old. Pausing on Heath momentarily I moved to the next item. It was a tub of some kind with a pack of papers on top. Dusting the lid, I took a closer look.

Leg wax! I remember pestering my mother for this

when I was thirteen or something. She had always refused saying a razor was safer. How she could think a sharp edge blade was safer than soft pliable wax was beyond me. I had skipped school one day to tag along with dad when he went to Rocky. When I was meant to be waiting in the ute I had managed to pop into the chemist and buy the wax with my own money. Looking at it now I don't recall ever using it. I think I was terrified that mother would catch me.

At this point any sensible person would have found the replacement tube of toothpaste and returned to the task at hand. The words 'wild woman of Borneo' still rang in my ears. I studied the wax. There was no use by date and the instructions appeared simple enough.

Suffice to say the bathroom door was quickly shut, the wax hurriedly warmed and with gusto my Borneo was slathered with warm gooey wax. Failing in sensibility doesn't mean an idiot, so I patted the paper strips onto the wax until it looked like I was wearing paper underwear.

Reviewing the instructions, I awaited the allocated time before peeling the paper back to reveal my new lawn. Gently with the longest nail that I had I flicked up the edge of a paper strip. I paused momentarily as I felt a small stinging sensation. In my wisdom I decided to place my toothbrush across my mouth. Something to bite down on in case this smarted a little too much. Smarted. What a stupid word for describing pain.

After several counts to three I finally ripped the paper from my groin area. In one foul swoop I had ripped the paper from myself and raised it in the air. Hey this didn't hurt as much as I thought. Quite painless really. Looking at the raised piece of paper I understood my calmness; there was nothing on it. No hair, no wax, nothing. Looking down I saw a lot of wax. Don't panic. Just breathe. The solution was easy. That piece of paper was faulty, the next will be fine.

It wasn't, nor was the next. All pieces came away free of anything. Now this was disturbing. Oh well, I scrapped my nail under the edge of the wax until I could get a fairly decent grip. Tugging at the wax I yelped. Thankfully mum and Tex were pre-occupied with the movie. Tugging again I yelped again, louder this time.

Oh, my goodness, what was I to do? Initially I had been standing, that had become tiresome, so I sat on the toilet seat to think. Okay, the thoughts came quick and fast, the answer was simple. All I had to do was heat the wax up so that it became pliable and easy to remove. Yes, I'm a legend.

Now how do you heat wax that is already on you? Simple! A hot bath. As I rose from the toilet, I felt a strange sensation. Looking down I saw the toilet seat coming with me. With a quick shove and a yelp, I corrected that issue. The bath took longer than I thought, I stood there waiting. No way was I going to sit on the toilet seat again.

Finally, the bath was sufficiently full and sufficiently hot. As I raised my leg to step into the bath I felt an irksome pull. With great difficulty I made it into the water. My skin rushed to a pinkish shade. Sitting in the warmth of the water I felt at ease. The wax was softening. Yippee!

I was even more heartened when small blobs of wax rose to the surface.

After sufficient time I tugged at the wax. To my horror the wax did not move. Well not without a lot of pain. Sitting up and looking down, I found myself in a new situation I had never been in before. Damn Gillian you are dumb! My struggle intensified while the water cooled. To remove the coolness, I pulled the bath plug to empty the water. Surely, that would help. There is only so much struggle you can achieve in the seated position, rising now seemed impossible. Oh, my goodness, I was stuck to the bathtub.

The shrill scream that followed was enough to draw attention. Tex was first at the door followed closely by mother.

'You okay my dear.'

Her motherly concern was daunting as she attempted to peer over Tex's shoulder.

'Yes mum. Would it be okay if I had a word with Tex, alone?'

'Sure baby.'

She left satisfied that her baby was in no harm at all. Little did she know. Sitting in the tub one hand over my breasts and another over my groin my eyes focused on Tex. Her eyes were intensely focused on me with a mixture of concern and amusement.

'Honey, why all the screaming.'

Describing my pain was not made more pleasant by the fact that I had to keep repeating myself due to the hearty laughter. Eventually as the goose bumps covered my body,

I was able to reveal the whole sordid affair. Thankfully she had thrown me a towel half way through the story.

'Gill, only you.'

Only me? Was that all Tex could say? No, there, there, everything will be fine. Tex sat on the toilet seat yet thought better of it when it attempted to follow her when she stood.

'A hair dryer. That is the answer.'

Tex mumbled more to herself than to me. Now as if the situation wasn't overwhelming enough. How could I let Tex see that area of me?

'Promise you won't look.'

'Gill!'

'Promise?'

'Whatever.'

Tex instructed me to lift my body with my arms while she warmed the area.

'If you push too early, you'll feel the sting. If you leave it too late, you'll feel the burn and I'm not meaning the burn of physical exercise.'

Section by section was warmed. Centimetre by centimetre I lifted my body. When Tex said now I pushed with all my might and discovered I was free. In my excitement I leapt into Tex's arms, hugging her with all my thanks.

'Um Gill. We aren't quite finished yet.'

'Yes, but I'm free.' Yes free, however now I had another feeling, something a bit more familiar. 'I need to pee.'

The laughter erupted from her mouth.

'Well sweets, you will need to hang on to that for a touch longer.'

Though the following details may be amusing for some I believe it is a moment in my life I would like to forget. And of all the people in the world to be there I had Tex.

'Don't look.'

The whir of the hair dryer stopped as Tex looked at me and took in my words.

'Gill, unless you want third degree burns from the dryer I need to look.'

'Well can't you look quickly then turn away? You know like a welder.'

'The only thing welded here are your legs to your pussy.'

Tex could be so rude at times. Surely it was not too much to ask to have my dignity kept a little intact.

'Tex, please?'

Lying half naked on my bed I lacked a little authority here.

'Do you want to do this yourself?'

As I considered her words, I realised she was peering into my nether regions making small scratch motions with a fingernail.

'Tex!'

This woman has no consideration for me and my dignity. An idea momentarily distracted me with thoughts of revenge; no make that justice, the justice I would impose on her.

'I'm warning you Gill.'

Tex's words were well composed and contained a scent of sternness.

'All I'm saying is that you could respect my dignity a little.'

'Your dignity huh?'

In what felt like slow motion, Tex stopped scratching at my nether region, looked me square in the eye and smiled. The smile was utterly disturbing, and then, it was followed by excruciating pain. In a single piece Tex had torn the wax away, and every hair my nether region ever owned.

The intensity of the pain overtook my body, though the joy of being able to spread my legs was remarkable. Such pain, such relief.

'That's the baldest badger I have ever seen.' Tex's smile intensified. 'And the angriest!'

Shyness took a back seat as I sprinted to the bathroom. The sheer exhilaration of finally being able to pee over-took any other emotion. Well at least for that moment. My mother was right. Razors are by far safer than wax, for so many reasons.

~ 23 ~

The park bench was on a rise overlooking the Sandgate pier. Seagulls played happily along the edge of the gently lapping water. Harry had been here before although it generally was with Clare. It was their place. A land of solitude. The very spot where each first declared their love for the other. This bench held many special memories. In her hand she held Clare's favourite flowers: daffodils. Soon she would set them adrift on the sea.

Today Harry wasn't dressed in one of her flash suits. No not today. Nor tomorrow either. Yesterday Harry had handed in her resignation. She had allowed a four-week transition period as was customary for someone in her position. In the last ten years of working there Harry had seen the magazine grow from a stumbling infant into a high-profile success. The owner had always praised her for the contribution she made saying it wouldn't have been possible without Harry. Over fifteen industry awards were achieved via the direct input of Harry. It was hoped the boss would be sympathetic to her resignation for personal reasons. He wasn't. Ten minutes after handing in her resignation Harry was escorted from the premises.

Squinting towards the sky Harry questioned the lack of permanency in life. She had miscalculated her importance at work. Harry was not the corner stone of its creation.

Like any employee she was replaceable. She had miscalculated the solidity of her marriage. Actually, she realised, she took it for granted. Always assumed it would be there, never once pondering the possibility of its loss.

Today, this bench, which had been the basis for many happy memories, was Harry's place to mourn. No evidence of Clare had been found up north. The police said they would investigate further though they fully believed she had committed suicide. Even so, no body was found. Clare's parents refused to communicate with Harry. They had made the police stop communicating with Harry too. Gay marriage was not recognised in Australia so technically without the partner's family consent, Harry was basically a nobody with no rights. The law saw her as a mere acquaintance, nothing more. So here she was at their own sacred site performing her own farewell to Clare.

Harry recalled the woman Sam. How this one woman had her feet planted in two different worlds. The wife and child contained in the home environment in Sydney. The many mistresses and one-night stands in Brisbane. Each world built on lies. Neither the true person. Harry considered herself and the worlds she stood in.

Somehow, she had always felt inadequate against Clare. Yes, she had become successful in her given field. Yes, she had provided for her family. Still, Harry wasn't happy. Sitting on this park bench Harry realised she had lost herself somewhere. When she had lost herself, no world was right.

Sam had failed her wife. Harry had failed hers. The difference was Harry recognised her failure, her weakness. It had come at a cost, a cost that she realised would always weigh heavily upon her, she vowed Clare's death would not be in vain.

Yes, Harry thought, she could blame the alcohol, although it had been her choice to drink. Reflecting now she realised it had been her oldest, and longest lasting, friend. It had been there through the bad times, especially her troubled youth. The good times too. It comforted her when she was sad and celebrated with her when she was happy. Day or night it had been there for her. Harry realised now that this friend was an addiction. An addiction that she used to escape her world. She needed to mourn the loss of this friend alcohol too.

Looking at it all now Harry realised she needed to move ahead. To find her real self and be comfortable with that. Tears welled in her eyes. They trickled down her face and onto the flowers. A petal wilted under the weight. She wished Clare was here.

~ 24 ~

It was the day before the festival and the men from Speckle went into overdrive. The morning sky was a little bleak and to be honest I was feeling the same. Butterflies swarmed in my stomach at the thought of being prominent on a float. I considered myself social but not that social. I wondered if that was strange or whether I was overreacting.

'Honey, I'm going over to Jed's to do the final touches on the float.'

Dad was chirpier than I'd seen him in a long time. Well other than when Charles the corgi won the championship. Mother seemed perkier too, she gave him a peck on the cheek while handing him a thermos. He was heading to Jed Zimmerman's workshop.

Jed Zimmerman was a boiler maker by trade. His welding prowess was in demand in the area. On cattle trucks, mining rigs and any other metal projects. In the last two weeks he had focused solely on the float and 'some extras' as my father put it. He was a true artist with metal as his medium.

'Ooh can I go?' Asked Tex.

She had been keeping a photographic journal of the festival's progress. Dad had let her take a few snaps the other day, though generally my mother was hogging her time.

'It's men's work love.' Father's face was soft as he offered Tex an apologetic smile.

I fully expected Tex to leap up and explain to my father that women are very much capable. She didn't. I wondered why. The possible scenario consumed my thoughts when I realised my father was speaking to me.

'Would you like to come Jilly?'

He looked half expectant, I wondered if this was out of some perverted civil courtesy considering I was the male and all. Sheesh I still can't believe my parents think that.

My eyes searched the room for an excuse; all I found was Tex's smirk.

'Oh no dear, Jilly needs to come with me for the fitting of her costume.'

Mother scolded father softly. He looked relieved and left. Now I was full of apprehension.

'Costume?'

I gasped. The thought hadn't even crossed my mind. Stupid, stupid me. I glared down Tex's chuckle. Mother tsked at me like we were children. You'd think that if I was going to be on a float, I may have considered what to wear. To be honest I didn't. Now I was concerned about what my mother had selected. Even worse, I considered what her Country Women's Group sewing club may have made.

I informed my mother I would meet her later as I wanted to contact Clare first. It had been a while since I had spoken to her. I thought I'd update her on my life. Surprisingly Tex had become more supportive, and we chatted every night in bed before going to sleep. Generally, she held me until I dozed off. It was becoming a comfortable routine. Surprisingly!

Like all of the times before, the phone rang out. With a sigh I dialled Harry. She'd been unavailable just as much as Clare so I rang her work.

'I'm sorry Ms Granger no longer works here.'

Was the only answer I could get to her whereabouts. My goodness what had happened to my friends? The friends who had been by my side since childhood. How could they all just vanish? Next, I tried Harry's mobile.

'Yep.'

Was the solemn response. That was so unlike Harry.

'Harry? Harry it's me.'

I paused expecting her to know then insecurity hit.

'Gillian!'

'Hey Jilly.'

Harry's voice was empty, detached, it made me panic.

'Harry? What's wrong? Are you okay? Is Clare okay?'

For the first time in my life I heard Harry cry. At first it was a little sniffle, then it was a torrential downpour.

'She's gone Jilly.'

'Gone. Where?' Where would Clare go?

She and Harry were one, never apart, never alone. Every thought flooded my mind. Every thought but one. Had she absconded with another woman? Did she change to liking men? Did she just leave? Did she kick Harry out? Why didn't she tell me?

'She's.' The pause was agonising. 'Well, they think she's dead.'

'Dead!'

Without knowing it I must have screamed the word for Tex came running from the bathroom. She barely managed to catch me as my knees turned to jelly.

'What do you mean dead?'

Tex lowered me to the floor.

'Who's dead?' Interrupted Tex who was squatting beside me now.

'How?'

The word could hardly call itself a whisper. There was no force or belief behind it. A great sob flew down the phone line. Followed by a muffled word.

'Possible suicide. They think it's suicide.'

'Possible? Who is they?'

'The police.'

'No that can't be true. Clare? No, not suicide. She helped on that youth hotline. No not Clare.'

The phone dropped from my hand, tumbled across the floor and came to rest against the floral lounge. Sorrow crushed my heart. Blood drained from my head and I melted into the floor. Tears blurred my vision, I did not care. Tex scrambled for the phone.

'Hello. Is that you Harry.'

I saw Tex's face turn ashen. I thought she was going to vomit, instead her eyes fell to me.

'Okay Harry. What are you saying? Is it true? Do you think it could be true? Well then, there is no hard evidence. I'll let you go, remember, I'll call later, okay? Hang strong Harry, we'll work through this okay?'

With that she dropped the phone and scooped me into

her lap. My mother found us there a few hours later. Tex was still rocking me. One hand pressed my head to her chest, the other encircled me as it had done since the call. It took a few more hours for mother and Tex to settle me. After three Valiums, I was able to be put to bed for sleep. Tex did not stray far from my side however she did manage to contact Harry while I lay in a disturbed slumber.

Harry explained the situation the best she could.

'It's all my fault Tex.'

'Don't say that Harry. Just give me the details first. What happened?'

'The police found her belongings on the top of a cliff. A well-known suicide spot.'

'No body?'

'No. No body.'

Tex could feel how distraught Harry was. Under normal circumstances I was the comforter, today Tex bravely took up the role.

'It's all my fault. I've been drinking too much. I was stupid. I betrayed her Tex. I betrayed Clare, the love of my life.'

'We all do stupid things Harry; you can't blame yourself.'

'I pushed her away therefore I wasn't there when she needed me the most.'

Harry's voiced fell an octave. A deep breath was taken before she continued. The tears rolled freely now.

'I hit her, Tex.'

'Shhh Harry.'

Tex's head hurt. Instinct told her to run. My crumpled

form made her want to stay. She had no idea what to say to Harry.

'All I pray is that one day you and Jilly will forgive me. I want to make this right. I'm going to get help, Tex. I'm going to rehab. I need to halt this addiction.'

Tex felt Harry's pain. No words of comfort would help. She knew the couple well. Had spent many hours with them. Not once had she seen Harry violent towards Clare.

'My God I don't know if I can survive without her.'

Harry remembered the cold steel of the gun pressed against her forehead. She had been too scared to pull the trigger. Her final words to Tex were simple.

'Forgive me.'

~ 25 ~

After travelling for three days, Clare was surprised Nikki was still with her. Initially Nikki had requested a ride to the next town, now many towns later they were still enjoying each other's company. They were currently in a no name town in New South Wales close to the Queensland border. The ocean was close, she could smell it. Nikki knew a friend here. Clare watched Nikki from the Kombi's window as she entered the bakery.

Nikki was what she would call a free spirit. Some may say hippy. Her clothes were free flowing as was her love for life. Nothing seemed to stress her, not even the lack of destination Clare had. This made Clare smile. Since she had left her life, she was free to wander wherever she desired. Harry preferred structure. Initially Clare thought she did too, now that was untrue. Her soul desired freedom. Freedom to roam and explore.

Nikki, in her own way, encouraged that within her. This free-spirited blonde thrived on lack of direction or destination. Returning to the camper Nikki had a jump in her step.

'Hey CJ. The baker mentioned a funky little festival that was taking place this week-end.'

'Really? Where?'

Clare enjoyed the sense of adventure.

'Queensland. Near some city called Rockhampton. Think we can make it in time.'

Typical Nikki thought Clare. Even though she had only known this woman for a matter of days, Clare knew that Nikki would assume that she was interested in the adventure. Plus, Nikki's sense of adventure never took into account the dynamics of a project, especially one that would be close to 900 kilometres.

'Sure, no problem.'

The words had fallen from her mouth. Let a new adventure begin.

~ 26 ~

The morning of the festival started a little overcast as was my mood. My body was heavy in a pain, unseen pain. Asleep next to me Tex had her arm wrapped about my waist. Her face had somehow aged overnight. I wondered if mine had too.

There was a small knock on the door as my mother poked her head through. She saw my eyes open, she paused. Possibly she saw the emptiness, the hurt, the loss of essence I felt. Mother approached anyway.

'Honey, you awake?'

Words failed me so I nodded. Memories of last night flooded my mind. Tears welled in my eyes.

'Shhh shhh baby.'

Mother patted my hair as she did when I was younger. She used to stroke it although now, there wasn't much left to stroke. A small smile wanted to break free at the thought.

'We all loved Clare. You know that don't you dear?'

Nod.

'The ladies and I will understand if you don't want to attend today.'

Mother had that look, the special one. The look of sympathy that was surely going to have a 'but' following it. It did.

'But it may take your mind off it, just for a moment. Clare would have wanted it that way dear.'

With that mother rose and left the room. Tex stirred a little.

'She gone?'

'Yes.'

Tex hugged me harder.

'You okay Jilly?'

She hesitated before speaking again.

'Well considering.'

'Maybe mum is right. Clare died, what, days ago?'

Alone, by herself, rattles through my conscience. I feel terrible. I wasn't there to talk with her, to comfort her. I recalled that last moment in the bar. Maybe, just maybe, I could have said something, done something that would have changed her choice.

'She disappeared days ago, there's no proof. They found her belongings and no body. Look, you just found out last night and are left in limbo. We know Clare. You know Clare. This just doesn't make sense. There's still hope.'

Tex snuggled into my back. In a vague way I think she was hoping we could skip this whole day. Instead I rose and went to the bathroom. While there I took another Valium for luck. Behind the door was the black suit bag that held my outfit for the day. The thought of it made me shiver. A hot shower failed to remove the chill I felt. Wrapped in a towel I attempt to view myself in the mirror. It's foggy so I swipe it with my hand. The shortness of my hair makes me smile. Tex had taught me how to wax it up.

For someone with long hair she knew a thing or two about short styles.

I 'm not one hundred percent, but I think the Valium was kicking in; hard. I smile at my hair. Teasing it is fun. The giggles take over my body, shaking it hard. My towel falls to the floor. Tex comes in, takes one look and laughs. As she bends to pick the towel up her hair grazes my arse. I laugh even louder. Tex struggles to wrap me up. Eventually she gives up and shrugs. Next thing I know she's climbing into the shower . . . naked! Though I shouldn't be surprised, she is quite beautiful. I must have been staring as she threw water in my face and told me to get back to my make-up.

Make up wasn't my specialty so under Tex's directions, from behind a sheet of water, I managed to make a face that vaguely looked unfamiliar. A wolf whistle came from the shower so I am pleased with my attempt. Grabbing the black suit bag, I scamper into the bedroom.

My outfit is slightly awkward. Not what I'd usually wear. I try to see myself in the small mirror. I twist my body this way and that. Peering over my shoulder to see if my arse looks ... well ... right.

'Hot. Damn hot!'

Such words were always quite flattering, no matter who they came from. Somehow coming from Tex, they meant a lot more. The number of women she has seen naked and she calls ME hot. What a compliment.

I spin round so she can see me fully. The sewing club had made me a pair of brown suede chaps with tassels, similar to the ones worn by Tex the morning I picked her up from the docks. That morning was the beginning of this journey. Hmmm. That morning seems so far away now.

Hooking my thumbs behind the belt buckle I'm relieved that I am allowed to wear something under the chaps, even if it is cut off blue jeans. Actually, they looked more like skimpy shorts and have no resemblance to jeans. The sewing club had debated whether I should wear a matching vest, they decided no, instead I wear a small brown suede bikini top with little matching tassels. In their wisdom I also have matching wrist bands: tassels and all.

Hand to her chin Tex stood looking, pointer finger tapping her cheek.

'It's missing something.'

Racing to the bed Tex dives across it. I must admit I did check out her arse in the black leather pants. Tight I think, in the same moment, I think maybe I shouldn't have Valium again. Then for some strange reason I think of strawberries. Mmm strawberries, that would be nice. Oh, dipped in chocolate. Mmmm chocolate. Tex's hand reaches to the bedside table where she removes her hat. As she returns to where I stand, she settles the hat on my head.

'Perfect.'

Then she kisses me.

'Is that how I look? Sweet!'

Sweet. Tex looks great so I must look great. Valium is fun, maybe I should have another. I'm placing it in my mouth as mum calls us. Did I just have one or two? Probably doesn't matter, I feel good. I look good. Hell yeah, I look good. Wow who would have thunk it?

Tex and I choose to skip breakfast. The plan was for us to meet the float at the staging area which was just outside of town. The float would carry us down main street where we were hoping for a crowd. Any crowd really. Five people would do. Yes, five would be great. Once we had completed the three blocks of main street the parade would head one kilometre out of town to the Lion's Park. A place where a merry fair was set up. A day of family fun my mother said. And later a dance party for the adults.

'Okay Gill where are the keys?'

I giggle as Tex's hand reaches out to me.

'Seriously Gill.'

Looking about my body I don't find any keys. I pat myself down just to make sure.

'I don't have them.'

'Gill this is no time for games. Where are the keys?'

Giggles surge through my body as Tex pats me down.

'I don't have them.'

'I gave them to you as we left the kitchen.'

All I could do was shrug and pat down my own body again. Tex makes us retrace our steps five times. We search the bedrooms, the lounge room, the kitchen, the laundry though I'm sure I hadn't been in there recently, and the car. It had been thirty minutes of hard looking so I thought it was time for another Valium. My hand got stuck in my back pocket looking for that sweet sweet tablet. Shaking the hand free I feel something slide down my leg. I look down amazed; it is the keys!

'That's it.' I declare. 'I had hung them over the back of my pants. They must have slipped in.'

Tex snatches them up.

'Lost in your crack, is that what you are saying? And you didn't even feel them?'

Surprisingly no. 'What a cracker of a tale!'

All Tex could do was shake her head and throw me into the passenger seat. It wasn't till we were close to town that I remembered the little tablet in my back pocket. In the car I squirm and wiggle, sadly it won't come out.

'Gillian, stop being childish. What are you doing?'

Tex tries to focus on the road. Like a scolded child I freeze.

'Nothing.'

Innocent face. I flick the visor down to ensure I have the right innocent face on. Then the giggles burst from me.

'Well thank goodness we're here. Come on Gill we're running a little behind schedule.'

Tex leaps from the car then circles around the front to open my door. How gentlemanly I think so I thank her with a smile and a quick peck on the cheek.

The float was beyond expectation. In fact, it took my breath away. A vast array of native flowers, four to six deep, encompasses the whole thing. Towards the front is a lush green grass the likes of which would only be found during a rainy season. Jed had constructed a mini windmill that took pride of place in the centre. As the wind silently pushed its blades fresh water was pumped into a low circular tank. Lush sugar cane stalks rustle in the same silent breeze. The cane traced the tail of the float.

Standing on the float itself, I felt transformed as if I was in another world. Standing eye level with the sugar cane gave the sensation that it flowed on forever, as if I could run through it. The aroma of the flowers was enticing.

'Gorgeous huh?'

Dad spoke; I couldn't see him.

'Down here.'

I look through a small patch of flowers to see a little hatch with my father's head poking out.

'It's beautiful dad. You driving today?'

'Sure am pumpkin. Couldn't let my girl go by herself. By the way, if you get hot feel free to jump in the water.'

The hatch shut concealing his laughter though I could feel the rumble of it seep up from the bowels of the float. Or was that the engine?

'Gill, you right? Need anything?'

Tex looks up from the edge. I shake my head. All this work, for me? I was gob smacked to say the least.

'The turn outs been great. Thirty floats have registered and people are lining the street. Up to four deep in some sections.'

Tex smiled apparently proud of the fact.

'You'll be last to go. Here come your escorts.'

From a nearby tent I spot a group of males. I recognised a few as local farm hands and jackaroos. None were gay as far as I knew. My mother was leading them.

'Gillian.'

Mother waves.

'Here are the boys. Betty just finished spraying them'

Each man was stripped naked to the waist exposing upper bodies that were now painted in a tanning lotion flecked with gold. Faux fur in a multitude of designs covered their legs in the form of animal trousers. Matching wrist bands helped to finish the whole look. Jed Zimmerman stood near his truck and as each man walked by, he handed them what looked like the skeleton of a horse head. The metal horse-head helmets sat neatly over each man's head and rested firmly on their shoulders. Luxurious manes hung loosely until the wind teased them into action. Then they swayed gently creating a mystical effect as if each one was half man half beast.

I blink twice making sure they aren't real horses. The float jumps into life and edges forward a few feet. The man-horses line up ahead of me and commence a gallop dance. My head surges and the world becomes a blur. Cheering rises to greet me, I have no idea where it is coming from. All I see is the greenness of the grass and the swaying of the cane.

Music bursts from a speaker on the windmill, I look up and gaze at the sun. Like electricity the music surges through my body. I begin to sway. To be honest I don't recall too much from there. I do recall getting wet, and splashing around. I think it was in a pond or something? At first, I thought I was daydreaming and playing in the yard as a child, then I wonder if I really was. Hmmm, oh my, did I swim in the windmill pond? Tex! Tex! Did you see me???

There was even a moment when I thought I saw Clare

in the crowd. I wasn't sure it was her, she looked different somehow though her face was carefree and full of laughter. When she saw me watching her, she raised her hands in mock applause then pursed her lips touching a finger to them as if our meeting was a secret. I marvelled at the fact that angels walk among us. Whether it was a dream or a reality, seeing Clare, even in my hazy state, made me smile and feel happy inside. So, I danced and the crowd cheered even louder.

Clare had found the festival to be awesomely fun. It was not till Gillian's float had passed her that she realised this small town was the butt of all her best friend's tales. Somehow none of those stories now rang true.

In a way it was exciting to see Gillian on the float. Her playing up the gay role though she did appear to be under the influence of something. During the dance party she had attempted to approach her one-time best friend though Tex never left her side not even for the cuties whistling at her. Even Nikky had made an attempt on Tex but was swiftly rejected. Clare was relieved when her travelling companion decided to depart with an interstate trucker. It was time she was on her own.

Watching the new day dawn from the Kombi Clare pondered the dynamics of their small group. Each had played a role that now seemed insignificant. Clare was gone and the world rolled on. Gillian had learnt to let go and Tex to hang on. From her pocket Clare drew an old well-worn photograph. It was of her and Harry on their first date. For years she had carried this little picture for it represented love, life and happiness. Now it offered no solace. For what was once full of life now represented nothing but emptiness.

A tear trickled down Clare's cheek as she lit one corner

of the photo. The flames rose slowly devouring the merging colours. As the final piece of ash crumbled from her finger Clare smiled to herself.

'Hey. I don't know if you remember me, we met last night?'

The girl peered around the edge of the sliding side door. Clare acknowledged her with a nod and smile.

'Well,' the girl paused in uncertainty. 'I was wondering if you'd like to join me for coffee?'

~ 28 ~

O.M.G. My head hurts bad. I try and recall the family fun fair or even the dance party however I can't manage it. Rolling over I feel out for Tex. She is nowhere to be seen. I moan, wallowing in my own misery. There is a sharp rap at the door. I call out to Tex to get it, there is no response.

Rising up my head feels three steps behind. It is not till I'm upright that I realise that I am at home, my home, in my own bedroom. Hmmm. Those Valium are good, too good. Mental note, NEVER have one again!

I manage to stumble down the stairs on the sixth, seventh or eighth knock. As I swing open the door, I see the delivery van drive around the corner. Crap Jilly, what if it was important? Scolding myself I squint at the midday sun. Midday? What the??? Stepping out to confirm the sun's position I trip over a plain wrapped parcel on the step.

Moving inside and dropping to the lounge I inspect the parcel addressed to Tex. It has the weight and shape of paper. Probably a men's magazine I muse as I toss it to the side table. Breathing in the silence I look around my familiar surroundings. Somehow, since the trip, the room lacked the warmth it once had.

I ponder whether it is because I had been away for so long. I ponder why the lounge no longer snuggles me the way it once did. I ponder why the air in the house now tastes so stale and the room so claustrophobic. Get over yourself Jilly. The room is stale because the house has been shut up for weeks.

Hearing a noise, I turn expecting to see Tex. Instead I am greeted by the neighbour's cat pawing at the closed window. Moving slightly, I startle the feline which bolts away. Strange cat really, it has never come around before.

Laying in the silence of my own home I attempt to recall the events of the last few days. In a way it is a blur. Damn those Valium, they were ever so sweet. Like strawberries. Mmmmm strawberries, they'd be nice right now. Oh, dipped in chocolate that's even better. Yes chocolate. I wonder where I could get some chocolate.

'Tex!'

The word leaves my lips before I even wonder why that is my first thought. Jeez Jilly, are you an invalid? As I rise, I hear a key in the door. Tex enters with her brow furrowed and her head down. In her hand is a box. Without acknowledging me she enters the kitchen. Like a puppy I follow, curious about the adventure to be had. Upon entering the kitchen Tex grabs a few items from the cupboard.

'What ya doing?' I ask playfully.

There is no response other than a muffled grunt.

'Want to grab something to eat?' I'm starving. I wonder when I last ate.

'You kidding me?'

Tex's face crinkles as it half turns to me. She doesn't

stop moving and loading things into her box. Next, she moves upstairs to the bedroom. Still confused I follow.

'Why not?'

With an audible sigh Tex stops what she is doing and turns to me.

'Do you not remember the last seventy-two hours?'

'Nope.' I cheerfully respond.

'Well ... I'll never forget them.'

With that Tex slams the box shut and practically sprints down the stairs and out the door.

Huh?

$$\sim 29 \sim$$

72 Hours Earlier at My Parent's House

'Holy frig Gill what do you want from me?' Speaking with frustration Tex look tired.

'One: I want my family back. MY FAMILY. Not yours. Two: I want to go home, I'm sick of playing this charade.'

Yes, a charade that is what it is Jilly, a charade. You go girl. Tell Tex the painful truths, she has no family and that is not your fault.

'End the charade: fine. Go home: okay. And they always have been and always will be YOUR family. Happy?'

Yes. I feel empowered by my choices. Damn my head hurts.

48 Hours Earlier in the Car

'What you are saying is that you think I'm a whore?'

Tex's hands strangle the steering wheel. Her back straightens and I can see some spittle in the corners of her mouth. Well I didn't say whore, I said slut. See Tex never listens.

'Whatever.'

Jilly how did you do this to yourself. I wonder how many more hours of this I have to put up with.

'Whatever? Is that it? So, miss high and mighty how did you come up with this enlightened idea?'

If Tex was a kettle her steam spout would have been

screaming. Instead her face turned crimson. Oh, this is easy.

'Well I don't recall you being around at the dance party. You must have been getting it on with one, or more, of the campers.'

'You are friggin kidding me? I was by your side ALL night, holding up your drugged arse.'

Tex spluttered, looked at the road then looked at me as if I was … what?? Hmmm, that was a new look.

'AND.' I emphasis to highlight my point.

'That bartender from Bundaberg. I saw her dropping you off in the morning at the motel.'

'What! Are you kidding me?'

The car brakes screech as the car swerves to the rocky shoulder. A horn blasts past. Tex repeats her words.

'You are kidding me?'

Nope.

'I saw what I saw.'

Aha check mate!

'Not that you care, you passed out and I spent the night in an uncomfortable motel chair watching you so you didn't choke on your own vomit.'

'And the girl?'

Get out of that one.

'I was so pre-occupied with you that I left my camera at the distillery. She was returning it.'

An unlikely truth is what I think. So is the glass smudged or is that my head.

24 Hours Earlier at My House

'So, if you love them and leave them, I assume you haven't left me, because I haven't fucked you yet?'

~ 30 ~

Looking in Hot Rocks' window was like looking into a fishbowl. It held a sense of repetitive calm and familiarity, Clare knew better. There was always the potential for staleness and a weird sense of strangulation as the oxygen vanished. This had once been her home away from home, now it was all a distant memory. She took in the patrons one by one until she came across a table that held so many memories.

Sitting at it were the ghosts of those memories. They were the same while somehow different. As Clare contemplated the option to enter the premises, she felt eyes settle upon her and approach.

'Hey angel. You don't want to eat in this dingy place, do you? It looks as though it's stuck in the past.'

Clare offers a pathetic smile to JoJo as he wipes a small tear from her face. Her reply is weak, hesitant.

'No.'

'I knew you'd return Clare bear.' Responds JoJo as he too looks through the window.

'Life has a way of changing on you.'

All she can do is nod. JoJo keeps his eyes focused in the distance as if he is speaking to himself.

'They will miss you.'

'Please don't ...'

Hushing her, JoJo pre-empts her next thought.

'Harry's doing okay. Finding new paths isn't always easy.'

No. Clare had come to realise that. As she turns, she feels JoJo's hand squeeze hers.

'Is Gillian working today?'

'No, I think she's been lost without you. She's not taking any calls and hasn't come back to work. Any chance you could see how she is? Come to think of it I haven't seen Tex either. Hmmm. You don't think the two of them have shacked up somewhere? What a laugh, as if that was even possible. Please, could you check in on her?'

A friend in need.

Even though the doorbell screamed at her, Gillian had little desire to answer it. Slumped in the couch, her body felt limp as if all the life had drained from it. Her world was in utter disarray. She had no answers. She had no-one to ask for help. Once upon a time she thought not having a partner was lonely, but this, this was a whole new level of lonely.

Seriously? Dragging herself from the couch she wondered what religious zeal made the person want to ring the bell for the fifth time. Didn't those people know when to give up and abandon a soul that couldn't be rescued. The bell screamed again as if demanding her to hurry. With a sigh Gillian swung open the door ready to be swamped with whatever gospel this person had prepared.

'Oh my! Clare! Clare you are alive.'

'Um yes, as far as I am aware. I haven't been gone that long, have I? You're such a nutter Jilly.'

Gillian stood there, hand still on the door for support, and stared at Clare, her long lost and supposedly dead friend.

'Gonna let me in you fool?'

'Yes!'

Gillian screamed as she dragged her best friend into her arms and started to weep.

'My, my, Jilly, what's the matter? Is it that time of the month or have you already hit menopause?'

Between sobs Gillian's words just came out as gasps and slurs. They were hurried and tumbled over themselves creating a language never heard before and one that couldn't be understood.

In her calming tone Clare led her to the kitchen, sat her down and started to make tea. Clare threw Gillian a box of tissues.

'Calm yourself down and we'll have a nice cuppa and catch up. Okay?'

Gillian nodded, sniffled, blew her nose and grabbed another tissue.

'Wow, look at your hair Jilly. That must have been a big decision for you.'

'Look at my hair? Look at your hair Clare.'

Both laughed and agreed that each had undergone a big change.

'To be honest Jilly, it makes me feel like a new person, like I am reborn.'

'You are. From dead to alive.'

'This dead thing again. What do you mean?'

Gillian tried to explain in sequence, but her story

jumped back and forth. Her thoughts and words all rushing to be out. She explained how the police thought she had committed suicide, how Harry had blamed herself and how her parents had pursued any lead they could find to prove her alive.

'Really? REALLY? You all thought I would top myself.'

A silent nod was her response.

'Oh, my parents. I'm going to have to call them. No, I'll go there next. They must be beside themselves.'

Another silent nod.

'It's just the end of a relationship, why would I kill myself? Shit happens in life. Flush and step forward as Tex always says.'

Gillian smiled at the thought of Tex's quote. Yes, flush and step forward.

'And I have stepped forward Jill. You would be proud of me. I've travelled, I've met new people.'

'And Harry?' I asked.

'Harry's a big girl Jilly. She can flush and step forward too.'

'She misses you.'

'She hit me.' Clare cast her eyes to the side, not in embarrassment, in thought. Then she looked Gillian in the eyes. 'I deserve better. It's about self-respect. I know I deserve better so why should I settle. No, I shouldn't.'

'I love the new Clare.'

'Me too!'

'You are so sure and positive. You were before but this is so much more.'

'I know, right?'

Clare appeared just as surprised as Gillian. They both laughed like they had always done. The moments lost seemed insignificant.

The topic of Tex eventually raised its head, it was actually in an off-handed way when Clare described how some random, she had picked up, Nikki, had hit on Tex without a single acknowledgement of her existence.

'It was like Tex was standing guard over you. And she seemed to take the job seriously. If it was anybody else, I would have said they were obsessive.'

'Wasn't she off playing around with all of the actually gay women?'

It seemed an obvious thing for her to do. Well obvious to me at least. Clare laughed before responding.

'You were so far gone I doubt you noticed anything all night. You were having a blast and were being hit on left and right. Dancing with whoever took your fancy for the moment. Don't you remember?'

Shaking my head, I tried to recall the night, my mind only came up with a blank. A blank with flashes of light.

'Tex was so awesome with my family.'

'And with you?' Prompted Clare, as intuitive as she ever was.

How could I answer that? What was there to say?

'It was just a fake relationship.'

'Was it? You seem... Well you seem upset that it appears over. And to be honest with you Jilly, it would explain a lot about Tex's actions, and might I say the way she looked at you, on that night. Damn, are you sure you don't remember? Or are you just blocking it out.'

'You're talking like I'm trying to sabotage a relationship out of fear of being loved.'

'Are you?'

Am I? How could Clare think I'm trying to ruin something that didn't truly exist. Yes, we had fun, we had
laughs and yes, she was there for me when I thought Clare
was dead.

'I thought you were dead.'

'I'm not.'

'No, you're not.'

'So, what has that got to do with your feelings towards
Tex.'

'What feelings?'

'You tell me?' Clare was ever so persistent.

'We had fun. We laughed lots. She made me feel good
about myself.'

'And?'

'And what? Do you want me to say I miss her?'

'Do you?'

Miss her? That cheeky grin in the mornings when she
grilled me before coffee. Before coffee, people! Who func-
tions before coffee? How she teased me incessantly over
my favourite television shows. How she spun her hat on
the bedpost. How she looked at me when I waxed myself
to a bathtub.

'God, I miss her.' I wailed aloud before realising it. Clare
smiled that knowing smile at me.

'I'm not gay Clare. We all know that.'

'Do you love her?'

'Oh Clare, I don't think I can live without her in my life.'

'Well then, you better invite her back into your life then.'

It sounded so simple. Clare always had practical solutions to everything. Solutions that sounded simple though in reality, could be frightening.

'What about you Clare?'

'Firstly, I need to visit my parents and put their minds at rest. Secondly, I think I enjoy this travelling gig, so I'm going to do more of that. It's truly a great way to find yourself. I just want to be happy Jilly. I don't think I have been for a long time.'

'Go be happy, you deserve it. Keep in contact though, because I miss you when you're not around.'

'And look at the trouble you get into when I'm not around.'

Laughter filled my kitchen.

~ 31 ~

Standing on the docks I have a sense of déjà vu. Once again, my stomach is performing flips so the knock, I deposit on the door is weak and half hearted. One moment I am full of confidence, the second I am not. Footsteps are followed by a voice. A voice so familiar I can touch it. Damn Gillian, what are you here to say?? Swinging open the door frames a familiar form.

'Gill?'

She looks surprised, I don't blame her I suppose. Be brave Gillian, be brave. Pausing I look past Tex.

'Are you alone?'

'Love them and leave them remember.'

The voice is dry without emotion. Her home is somehow different from when I last saw it. She catches me gazing about.

'I changed careers.'

She is somehow different.

'Oh.'

That's all that will leave my mouth. Oh. How pathetic. I have so much to say, words fail me, then I remember the parcel. I offer it like a peace pipe. Noticing it is open Tex looks at me.

'Don't get enough of your own mail, huh?'

'I read the articles you wrote. I never knew you had such talent. They were amazing.'

'You read them? My talent, huh. I thought you said I only had one talent.'

Ouch, that stung yet I deserved it. Oh, Jilly how did you stuff things up so much? I can't even remember the hours that caused this. Instead I shake my head and blubber out how awesome the articles are. I feel like some sort of groupie. Tex informs me that both magazines were so impressed they had offered her freelance work. Her eyes sparkled as if she ... as if she was ... I couldn't quite put my finger on it. I had never seen Tex with that sparkle.

'I'm sorry, it was the Valium. I don't recall a thing about those seventy-two hours. Tex, what...'

I was trying to form the question in my mouth.

'Don't Gill. Please don't.' Her eyes plead in a way I had never seen before.

'But.'

Her eyes beg me to stop.

'Why haven't we seen each other since returning?'

Barely a whisper her voice is husky in response. 'You know why.' The words crackle in insecurity.

'The house is empty without you.'

My life is empty without you is what I want to say. Just breathe Jilly, you can do this. Looking at her face, her utterly beautiful face, I need answers.

'Mum rang and asked for you. I didn't know what to say. She still thinks we live together.'

'Still worried about what your mum thinks Gill?'

Standing barely a few inches from me, Tex's eyes pierce mine.

'What do you think? What do you want?'

Though the words are simple, I know the words hold so much more. I wonder what it is I'm doing here. I wonder what it is I truly want. I reflect over the months that have passed. I reflect over the life gone by. I reflect on the laughter and good times I have shared with this person. This person! Is that all I can call her.

'Tex.'

'Yes.'

Her eyes pierce even deeper trying to find the truth themselves. Hell, I don't even know the truth.

'I miss you.'

'Is that it? Get a dog.'

'Tex, I miss the way you make me laugh. I miss the way you fill a room with your personality. I miss the way you make me breakfast. Most of all I miss the way you look at me.'

'Get a droopy eyed dog then.'

Tex shrugs and turns her back to me. She appears to be tidying things on her side table. Does she know how hard this is? Does she know what I'm trying to say? DO I know what I'm trying to say?

'Tex!'

'What Gill?? You want someone to follow you around, to make you feel good when you feel sad, to fix your problems??? Well you know what, I have needs too.'

The veins on her neck bulge. Her voice holds anger, her

face holds something else. So, I make one last ditch effort to be totally honest.

'I can't be roommates with you because I want you. There I've said it. I want you more than I have ever wanted anything or anyone in my life. I want to wake up to your beautiful face every morning. I want to kiss your amazing lips every moment of every day. I want your arms wrapped tightly around me when I'm happy or when I'm sad or when I'm scared. Most of all I want you all to myself.'

I take a step closer, then Tex pulls me firmly into a tight embrace. What can I say?

'Besides, I owe you an anything.'

Her look is inquisitive. 'Anything?'

Dash Starkey

Born and raised in Brisbane, Australia, Dash Starkey melds imagination with personal experiences to create lively stories. Paying homage to the state of Queensland in every book, with most having a home base of Brisbane, the stories have a personal feel, even when the characters travel the world.

Dash mulls over a novel started over 25 years ago, along with other works in the pipeline. Free time is spent between writing and van life. Dash's two greatest passions outside of family. Travelling with Elle in an old Toyota Hiace called Howie, Dash has many more adventures, and disasters, to divulge.

Backed by years of experience as a technical writer Dash Starkey has written articles for several magazines across the world, including Mountain Biking Australia, Australian Cyclist, Guitar (US), Bass Guitar (US) and Game Informer. Articles have also appeared in trade magazines and international inhouse magazines.